TWISTED LIES

SEDONA VENEZ

"It has been said, 'Time heals all wounds.' I do not agree. The wounds remain. In time, the mind, protecting its sanity, covers them with scar tissue, and the pain lessens. But it is never gone."

—Rose Kennedy

PROLOGUE

SINTHIA

MANHATTAN. Present Day. W.C. (With Core)

HOW THE HELL DID THIS SHIT HAPPEN?

I fucking hate him, but I want him.

It was sick and sordid, and I couldn't tell what this really was. I only knew when I was around him, he suffocated me with his twisted lies and dirty secrets, only to cruelly resuscitate me. And shamefully, I loved it.

Core stepped forward, caging me alongside his desk, making sure my body was flush against his. "Ready to fuck, Sin?" he whispered in my ear.

I sucked in a breath as his hard bulge pressed into my stomach. Mesmerized, I watched his hand reach out. His callused fingers slid down my cheek before his thick thumb dragged across my bottom lip and penetrated the barrier of my wet, pouty lips. My body jerked at the sensual intrusion.

Honestly, I wasn't really sure how to process the touch of a man again. It'd been so long I'd forgotten just how good it felt to have a strong hand touching me.

He scowled. "Sin, don't move," he demanded huskily while

grabbing the back of my head with his other hand. "Show me how much you want this, how much you want me. Lick it like you want it, darling."

I should stop him before this goes any further.

I knew I should, but my body thought otherwise. I was high off his lies and drunk off his hate. Now there was no way out. On cue, I ran my tongue along the length of his thumb as if it were his shaft. When he growled with pleasure, a tremor pulsed through my body as my cunt contracted.

Jesus, I'm so fucked.

Our mouths were a breath away. The desire and tension were almost more than I could take. Abruptly, he removed his thumb, still cupping the back of my neck, pulling hard on my hair, before his lips settled across my mouth. My breath caught, my mind undecided as to whether I should pull back or allow him to delve further.

Who am I kidding?

There was no allowing. I was Core's possession, and the cocky bastard knew it.

I moaned sensually as his tongue curled around mine, demanding it come out and play. He awakened a need that lay dormant in the pit of my stomach, a need only he could satisfy.

He skated his hand down and squeezed my hip while his eyes were fixed on mine. "I want you. Now," he growled.

My pulse raced, and my body trembled with want. He was crumbling my resolve. Diabolically, he stripped me bare emotionally, leaving me vulnerable and raw to the bone. He was revealing a piece of me that would be better left hidden. The message was clear. He knew what I needed, and he would give it to me if I took the leap of faith.

He smiled like the devil reincarnated as he released me and sat on the leather chair with his legs splayed. My stomach rolled with anxiousness as I leaped into the pits of scorching hell by pushing up the hem of my dress before straddling his legs. I shook my hair slowly as I rotated my hips. He grabbed my ass hard, stilling my movement.

I trailed my fingers over his chest. "Then take me, McKay, until there's nothing left." I leaned in toward him and bit his lower lip.

He gave me a bad-boy smile, causing my stomach to flip-flop like I was on a roller coaster.

"Sinful." He licked my bottom lip slowly. He pulled back with his eyes locked on to me with a power that left me breathless. "Are you mine?" he asked gruffly.

My heart raced with sickening excitement. I knew he was evil, lust, and darkness personified. He should have terrified me, but he didn't because I was just as fucked up in the head as he was.

"Always," I whispered.

"I'm never letting you go, Sin." Tilting my head back, he kissed me hard. "What I claim, I keep."

I was a spider trapped in his web.

"Now get on your knees," he ordered in a brusque tone.

This was it—the moment of truth that would seal my destiny. Self-preservation finally kicked in.

My mind screamed like a banshee, *Run, Sin! Tuck your ass and run!*

My body tightened, preparing to run away as if a horde of paparazzi was nipping at my stilettos.

Core's cold gray eyes narrowed. "I'm a hard-hearted, ruthless motherfucker who doesn't know shit about love or relation-ships." He pulled me forward, one hand taking a firm hold of my wrists, while his legs forced my knees apart. "And neither do you." His free hand ripped off my panties. "Perfection is complete fantasyland bullshit."

His hand slid against my pussy, and two fingers pushed inside, stretching me open. I moaned as I clenched around those fingers tightly.

"See, darling?" He smiled knowingly. "That's our reality. It's raw, wicked, and wild—a connection on a level very few will ever have or could even dream of."

I didn't have it all figured out. What I did know was Core was no Prince Charming, and I, for damn sure, wasn't a princess. There would be no fairy-tale ending for us. It would be hard work, and more importantly, it would be real. Life couldn't be all about tiaras and knights riding in to save the day.

Damn it! I would rewrite my fucking story and leap into the black abyss on faith alone because I wasn't looking for forever.

I licked his lips, unzipped his pants, and wrapped my hands around his hard cock before squeezing hard. He hissed as he relaxed against the soft leather chair, watching with intensity as I slid to my knees.

This was my give. This was his take.

And there was no going back.

Till death do us part...

❧　I　❧

SINTHIA

MANHATTAN. Past. B.C. (Before Core)

I BLINKED BACK HAPPY TEARS. ME, THE GIRL FROM THE OTHER side of the tracks, had been accepted into my dream school. And naysayers like Kyle Fillion—my worthless ex-boyfriend—could kiss my ass.

Even after all this time, I couldn't believe his hateful words still hurt like a motherfucker.

The truth of the matter was I wasn't sure what I was more ashamed of—that I had been so weak back then when we were together, or that he'd proven it so easily when I allowed him to trample my heart and pride without even fighting back.

My heart raced just thinking about that ego-bruising night. *No. That's ancient history, and I'm not that naïve girl anymore.*

I brutally pushed down the emotional pain.

Fuck Kyle, and fuck love!

Horns honked loudly, mercifully jolting my thoughts back from an impending descent into depression. I sucked in a lungful of stale, humid air as the cab driver cursed and hit his own horn.

He mumbled under his breath while tapping the steering wheel as we sat in heavy Manhattan traffic.

Damn, I should have just taken the subway.

I bit my bottom lip, staring at the bumper-to-bumper gridlock. I was going to be late for work, again, and Grace was going to lose her shit. I pushed a few wisps of blond hair off my face, then touched my neck.

"Great," I muttered.

The ringing of my cell snapped me from an almost frantic tirade.

"What's up, Jade?" I smiled goofily.

Only Jade could bring me back from the brink of panic.

"What's up?" She paused dramatically. "My girl, Sinthia Michaels, has arrived! That's what's up. I'm so happy for you, Sin. I knew you would get in!" Jade screamed.

Knowing her, she was probably doing her happy dance in the middle of Manhattan. It was so cute how gleeful and excited she was for me.

"Well, I wasn't as sure. Getting into fashion school was a long, frenzied, competitive process," I responded.

Jade laughed. "Please. You worry too damn much. You're a super-talented clothing designer. One day, your hot collection will be parading down the runway during fashion week. And I'll be holding court in the front row, salivating over all the clothes I get to snap up first."

I chuckled. "Well, thank you for being my living mannequin."

I designed most of my clothes using her as my sounding board. She was patient, enthusiastic, and always there for me. She was everything a best friend should be.

What other high school girl would allow a budding designer to create her prom dress? Only Jade would take such a risk, and it had paid off. The dress had been all anyone could talk about at prom. The excitement over my design had given me the extra boost of confidence to pursue my dream.

I wanted to design clothes for a living. According to Grace, it would be a complete waste of fucking time. Just thinking about her constant verbal barbs filled me with anger, pain, and fucking resentment. Her emotional abuse would have broken me by now if it weren't for my dad's love and nurturing.

Damn it! I miss him so much.

I blinked back the tears. It had been nearly a year, and I still couldn't think about him without breaking down in a sobbing fit. Just trying to cope with his death had been rough on me. He had been my rock. Dealing with the psychological bullying from Grace had made coping with his untimely death and the trials of living without his protection nearly impossible.

But I was taking it one day at a time, and thanks to Jade's moral support, I was surviving. Jade had been my best friend and my biggest fan since high school. We complemented each other despite the fact that Jade and I were just so...different.

Jade was the daughter of Ariana Bellisario—a philanthropist, heiress, and successful businesswoman—making Jade a member of the illustrious group of New York socialites whose monthly allowance was more than what most people would make in a year.

I, on the other hand, grew up in a middle-class family. They had been happy as shit when I'd received a scholarship to attend the ultra-elite private high school whose students included the children of celebrities and foreign dignitaries.

Our differences didn't end there. Jade was beautiful and lithe, with shocking apple-green eyes. My olive-colored skin and features were more exotic—or what guys would call sensual. I could live with that description, but it was my tight, curvy body that caused me angst—well, that and the fact that I had more ass and breasts than should be allowed on any woman unless her life-long ambition was to be a very well-paid stripper.

Jade was my bestie and my partner in crime. When she needed me, I was there just like she'd be for me. It'd been that way from the first day we met as freshmen in high school, and it would always be that way.

Jade jarred me out of my thoughts by screaming at the top of her lungs, "Sin! Are you fucking listening?"

I clutched my pearls. "Shit! Do you have to be so damn loud?" I snapped.

The cab driver scowled at me in the rearview mirror.

"Okay. Grumpy much?" Jade responded dryly.

I sighed. She was right. I should have been bouncing up and down with excitement. It was a huge life goal of mine to attend one of the best fashion schools in the country. I'd worked so hard for this day, and it was finally here.

"Now, how in the hell are you going to break the good news to Grace?" Jade asked.

And there it was, the motherfucking killjoy—my mom. My fingers twitched. Anxiously, I straightened my crisp oxford shirt and then smoothed down my black skirt as if I were somehow being scrutinized by her unforgiving glare.

"I don't know." I bit my bottom lip. "I'm on my way there now. Any suggestions?"

I felt sick to my stomach just from thinking about the inevitable confrontation. Our relationship had never been good. Grace wasn't...well, motherly. Okay, the woman was plain narcissistic. She always had been, and she always would be.

"Number one—don't let her mindfuck you, Sin. Stay true to your plan. You're going to school." Jade's voice hardened. "You've worked too damn hard to let her dash away your dream."

It hurt like hell to admit it, but I'd never gotten the sense that Grace loved me, and I damn sure never could do anything right in her eyes, no matter how hard I tried. And believe me, I'd tried. It was fucking embarrassing how hard I'd worked to be everything she expected me to be—flawless. I'd even dyed my long, naturally auburn hair blond like hers, which looked utterly ridiculous with my olive-colored skin and exotic features. What was worse was the sheer disdain in her eyes when she'd seen it. In comparison to her ethereal, porcelain looks, I wasn't pretty enough or thin enough or smart enough. I just wasn't enough... and, frankly, the truth hurt like a motherfucker.

I sat stiffly, clenching my fingers around my leather handbag. "You're right. I have to be firm with her. I want to go to school. I just haven't quite figured out how in the hell I'm going to pay the tuition."

"Sin, just tell her you earned her help with paying the tuition. You've been busting your ass while assisting her in that over-priced teahouse for months. For fuck's sake, she claimed she couldn't afford to pay you, but then she went out and bought a luxury vehicle with cash." Jade scoffed. "God, that woman is worse than my piece-of-shit father."

My lips pursed just from thinking about how Grace had burned through the money from my dad's life insurance settle-ment on extravagant purchases. Including a new condo with a homeowner's association fee that was more than what most people paid for their monthly mortgage. To make matters worse, she was living way above the income generated from her new teahouse business.

I ran my fingers through my hair. "Thank you for giving me the swift kick in the ass I needed. You're right. I must take care of me. God knows, if I don't, she damn sure won't."

"That's what friends are for," Jade responded.

I sighed. "I'll call you later."

"Okay. Remember, I have an audition today, but I'll be home right after. I have a feeling this is going to get real ugly, so give me a call, or even better, stop by."

"Shit! I'm sorry. I forgot your big audition is today. Get off the phone. You need to get your mind right. No more talking about my dysfunctional family." I sighed heavily. "Thank you, Jade. I don't know what I would do without you."

Jade laughed huskily. "Shit, you were there for me when I

went through my hot-mess phase, and now it's my turn to be there for you. Just call me, no matter what, okay?"

"Okay. Concentrate on getting that part." I hung up, pulling a compact out of my handbag, checking myself in the mirror.

I flipped my hair over my shoulder, touched up my mascara and lip gloss, and then fiddled nervously with my pearl necklace and earrings. They were gifts from Grace for my eighteenth birthday in lieu of the new sewing machine I'd asked for.

My body jerked from the sharp stop in front of Grace's teahouse. After paying the cab fare, I hopped out. My hands trembled while running them along my tight pencil skirt, trying to get out the nonexistent wrinkles. I froze, realizing I was on my way to what Jade called my *level ten panic attack*. Blowing out a breath slowly, I counted to ten before making sure to cover my one act of rebellion—the tattoo that read *Sin* in cursive letters on my wrist. If Grace were to see the tattoo, she would clutch her damn pearls, screaming that proper young ladies—more importantly, her daughter—didn't get tattoos.

My hands clenched and unclenched while I stood in the middle of the busy sidewalk, jostled by irritated New Yorkers. *I can do this. I can go in there and tell her I am fucking done with her shit.* My heart was racing as if I'd just run a marathon. *I need to get my shit together.*

Okay, it's go time.

I straightened my skirt once more. Pushing my shoulders back like Dad taught me, I marched into Grace's over-the-top Victorian teahouse like I was going to war—because I was, and it would be a bloody one.

Immediately, I gagged from the overpowering rose incense in the anteroom as I stared around the packed, twenty-seat establishment. *Great!* Now I would have a full audience when she went ballistic.

I skirted around the guests milling about and admiring the Victorian-style architecture and furnishings that had cost a fortune—and I should know. I had been an unwilling participant in antiquing with Grace on many long Saturdays. She had insisted everything had to be perfect when she opened her teahouse, which was located on the Upper West Side. Moving farther into the parlor designed with dark wood tables, exposed brick, and the white pressed-tin ceiling, I slowed my pace as I took a few minutes to gather my waning strength before proceeding into the dimly lit dining room with the tall, fringed floor lamps.

My stomach clenched when I saw her, and as usual, not one strand of her blond hair was out of place in her tight bun. Her apple figure—large chest, small waist—was encased in a tight black sheath as she strolled between tables, greeting guests with a beauty contestant's smile and a flawless facade. But her frosty blue eyes told the true story. She was drunk...again.

How could a woman so beautiful be such a damn mess?

Between her binge drinking until she blacked out and her disappearing every night before closing and not returning home until the next morning, she had been more erratic and self-destructive than ever. The strange behavior had been going on for weeks, and I was tired of being her free labor. This was her damn business—a business she'd forced Dad to work extra hours to help her attain, a business that had ultimately cost him his life.

Grace tripped, and I grimaced.

Shit!

This was the last thing I needed right now—to go toe-to-toe with her when she was all liquored up. Like a bloodhound, she sniffed out my presence, pinning me to the spot with a glacial stare.

"Good," she snapped loudly. "You're early for once." She pointed impatiently to the tables. "We're short-staffed today. I need you to work the tables. I'm expecting a big crowd." She jammed her hands onto her narrow hips, looking me up and down with undisguised disgust. "And stay away from the pastries. You're busting at the seams in that skirt."

The guests snickered into their dainty teacups.

My mouth dropped open in shock. *What. The. Fuck?*

Effectively dismissing me, Grace returned to flitting among the tables.

I rolled my shoulders to relieve the pressure.

Enough! I wasn't going to let her bully me. There would be no running away in shame or purging everything I'd eaten to compensate for my inadequacies. *The madness stops now.*

"Mom!" I screamed over the clinking of teacups.

Grace's head whipped around. Her lips thinned. "My name is Grace—not Mother, not Mom. How many times do we have to go over this?"

My stance widened. "*Grace*, we need to talk."

Her eyes narrowed. "Be quick about it."

Okay, if she doesn't want to handle this politely, then I'm not going to make it easy for her. "I quit," I snarled. "Is that quick enough for you?"

Her serene mask slipped. "In my office," she hissed before snapping her fingers at me. "Now!" She swayed off toward her office with her stilettos tapping angrily against the wood floor.

By the time we stepped into the white-on-white, expansive space with a silver, glass-topped desk, I was practically grinning, enjoying the fact that her facade had slipped. Now her customers had caught a glimpse of the real monster she was. Grace slammed the door. Photos of her faded beauty queen–contestant era crashed to the floor.

She stalked toward me. "This is my damn business, and you will treat it with respect, young lady!" she screamed while pointing in my face with erratic, jerky motions.

I flinched. She smiled smugly.

Fuck!

The stench of alcohol on her breath made me want to hurl.

"Respect?" I looked at her incredulously. "You belittle me in front of a roomful of strangers, and you want to talk about respect?" My jaw tightened. "I've been accepted into fashion school, and I'm going," I snapped.

Grace crossed her arms. "Well, that's not happening. You will work here until you find someone from the right family to take pity on your ass and marry you." She stared at me coldly.

I couldn't believe that growing up, all I'd wanted—no, all I'd *needed*—was to be loved by her. It was a bitter pill to swallow that she would never love me, but I had to let go.

"No, Grace, I'm not. I'm going to school. It's what I want, and more importantly, it's what Dad would want."

She glared at me with contempt. "Well, he's not here, is he?"

My mouth tightened. "No, he isn't!" I shouted. "Dad died from working himself to death to give you all the superficial bullshit you demanded, like some pampered princess." My mind reeled with distaste at how cavalierly she was acting, as if Dad's death had meant absolutely nothing. Briefly, I closed my eyes to calm down, and then I stared at her pointedly. "Look, I'm not here to ask for your permission. All I ask is that you help me with tuition for the first semester."

She scoffed. "Not happening."

I shook my head, disappointment clear on my face. "Maybe I'm expecting way too much from you. I was hoping for a little happiness or maybe some compassion." Tired, I ran a hand over my forehead. "Fuck, I'm so damn delusional."

Grace was the only family I had left, and even when she cut me down every day with her hurtful words, I would stay. It was a fucked-up dependency. Maybe all the years of her pounding into my head that I wasn't worth shit had finally taken root, like poison ivy tainting my soul and mind. Maybe I was just too fucked in the head to leave. *I mean, who in their right mind lives and works with someone who doesn't like them—let alone, respect them?*

I sighed heavily. The answer was abundantly clear—me.

I was done being walked on and making sacrifices for a woman who didn't give a shit about me.

Grace's eyes were vacant. "My answer is no, Sin. I'm not

giving you a damn dime," she snapped. "Besides, I need you here to help me run the teahouse."

I opened my mouth, closed it, and then repeated the procedure. "You can't be serious?" I glared at her. "I'm not a child, Grace. I'm eighteen years old. I've spent all my life being exactly what you want—good grades, no drugs, and flawless. After Dad died, I helped you build your business. I did it because I love you, but that doesn't mean you get to make my decisions for me or judge me when I don't agree with you or don't want to be your minion."

Her well-groomed eyebrows lifted. "I will not use my money to pay for some bullshit fashion design school. Besides, I've seen your tasteless clothes, and you're not that talented. Believe me, you will *never* make it."

I stared at her, wondering when she became such a hateful, judgmental bitch. "I'm not working here, and I'm going to school," I sneered.

She went stubbornly silent with pinched lips. "Fine. You are no longer welcome in my home. Consider yourself cut off from me."

I swallowed hard. "Since you've never loved me, Grace, there's not much to miss."

Her face went rigid. "You ungrateful little tramp!"

"What the hell should I be grateful for?" I laughed bitterly. "I spent so long putting everything you want and need first that I stopped mattering, even to myself. I'm not even a functioning person. I'm just a shell." I was done with Grace and her verbal abuse. I needed the toxic waste out of my life. It was time to start anew.

"Good-bye, *Mother*."

Her mouth dropped open in shock. "You'll never make it," she screeched. "You'll be back, begging for forgiveness."

My face tightened. "I wouldn't hold my breath if I were you."

I turned on my heel and walked out of the office and back through the teahouse. I was never planning on looking back.

Stepping onto the sidewalk, I ripped the pearls off my neck, staring as they bounced and rolled across the pavement and into the gutter, exactly where they belonged. I glanced up at the beautiful clouds as I exhaled. This was my new start, and I wasn't going to waste another damn second thinking about my dark past again.

❧ 2 ❧

SINTHIA

JADE FLUFFED UP MY HAIR, DETERMINED TO GLAM ME UP. I rolled my eyes at her. I guessed it wasn't enough that I had on my hottest outfit. She pursed her lips, beholding her masterpiece —me.

"Where's your party face?" Jade asked.

I yawned. "What are you talking about? This is my party face."

"The hell it is. You look like you're about to curl up as if you were some damn cat." She rolled her eyes. "Get your party face on, damn it. We're celebrating. We're going to turn it up tonight. Tabitha, the Iron Dragon, has finally acknowledged how talented you are."

I pumped my fist unenthusiastically before sliding down against the leather back seat. I'd only had a few hours of sleep, and this was all the zeal I could muster. It had been an exhausting day—or rather, it had been an exhausting year. After I'd enrolled in design school, my life had gone through a tornado of events—from moving into Jade's new luxury apartment in Manhattan to interning during the day for Tabitha Thorp, the temperamental and eccentric celebrity fashion designer. All the while, I'd been working a dead-end job at night.

I was mentally and physically drained.

Even with the steady paycheck coming in, I still hadn't been able to keep up with the tuition. It had been heartbreaking when I'd had to drop out of school after only nine months. I'd really thought my dream was over, but surprisingly, Tabitha had thrown me a lifeline, offering me a full-time job. The job offer had turned my life from negative to positive.

Even though Tabitha was a perfectionist and a pain in the ass, I'd learned a lot from her, and I'd eventually gained her trust and formed a strong friendship. Our friendship had forced me to push my creative process and clothing designs to the next level. So today, when she'd called me into her office and told me she was giving me a small space to sell my designs in her upscale SoHo boutique, I'd nearly fainted from excitement.

"Heads up, your stalker, Jaxon, is going to be at the club tonight." Jade dug in her designer handbag, pulled out lip gloss, and handed it to me. "Here, put this on and plump up those gorgeous lips."

I gave her a sidelong look while grabbing the tube. "Jaxon? How does he know I'm going to be there?"

"Because I told him." Jade ran her fingers through her hair. "It's time for you two to stop circling each other with your exhaustive flirting. Get to the damn fucking already."

Kirby, who worked as Jade's chauffeur, chuckled.

I jabbed her in the side. "Will you lower your damn voice?"

"Ouch! What?" she screamed, giving me the evil eye. "Kirby's like family."

"And it's not flirting. It's foreplay, which you know nothing about," I said.

"Foreplay doesn't last for three months. That's as annoying as a guy going down on you for more than fifteen minutes. Enough already." Jade pursed her lips. "It's been months since you've had sex. All that work and no fun has made you one cranky bitch."

I grimaced. "It hasn't been that long."

"Bullshit."

I counted in my head. *Shit. She's right.* Maybe it was time.

I shook my head. "I'm not sure I want to have sex with him."

I twirled my hair, staring out the window at the New York traffic whizzing by. I wasn't opposed to filthy, hard sex with Jaxon, but it would only be on my terms. My terms were nonnegotiable—no attachments and absolutely no relationships. I didn't have time for it. These were my rules of engagement. The knowing gleam I'd seen in Jaxon's eyes told me he was willing to play by my rules. He wanted me. I was his current fixation, the new flavor of the month, and he craved a lick before he moved on to the next woman.

The situation should have been golden, but something about him niggled at me, warning me to stay away. Maybe I was just annoyed that he was what I called a *chameleon*. By night, he would play gigs like some starving musician, and by day, he was the only son of a filthy rich family, who were waiting for him to get his shit together and join their prominent law firm.

Maybe I was just tired of men like him—cocky, wealthy, spoiled, and privileged. Their entire lives had been planned for them, and those lives didn't include getting serious with women like me with no pedigree. Men like Jaxon would only fuck women from the wrong side of the tracks, and when they got bored, they would settle down with the ice-princess socialite women their parents had picked out for them from the day they were born. I'd learned the hard way that relationships, love, and commitment didn't mean shit to affluent, overindulged people like him.

"Okay... Well, maybe some deep-throat action?" Jade asked matter-of-factly.

Kirby swerved.

"Uh...that's still considered sex." I sighed heavily. "I don't know." I arched a brow. "Don't you think it's creepy that he's been showing up at every club I'm at? It's like he's got a damn GPS on my ass."

Jade shrugged. "Creepy? No. Focused? Yes. He wants you—bad. According to his schedule, you should have been checked off on his 'already fucked' bucket list." She lifted a brow. "Would it be so horrific to try him out? You know"—she waggled her eyebrows saucily—"to take the edge off?"

"You do know he's not some car I can take out on a test-drive?"

Jade regarded me, totally perplexed. "Why the hell not?"

I couldn't stop my laughter. "Okay, you're right. I could test-drive him, but... I don't know." I bit my lower lip. "There's something about him I can't put my finger on."

Jade's eyes softened. "Sin, you've got to get over Kyle."

My brows came together in a puzzled frown. "I have."

Jade stared.

My gut started churning in that familiar way when I thought of Kyle. He had been my first everything—first boyfriend, first lover, first mistake. And just like clockwork, the self-loathing began to slither through my veins like poison.

I sighed heavily. "All right, fuck it, I haven't."

I cringed just from thinking about the emotional mess I was after Dad died. I had been weak. Mom had turned her back on me, leaving me searching for something I didn't understand, even now. I was like a junkie, cut off from my next fix of love, and I'd been left to die a slow, emotional death. Adrift, I'd shut down my heart, but Kyle had wanted in, and I'd let him in because my delusional ass thought he was worth it. But A.K.—After Kyle—I decided there was only one way to avoid the pain of love. Close off my heart permanently. It was no longer open for business, and I planned on keeping it that way.

Jade studied me, worried. "There's no shame in admitting it. He was a fucked-up high school crush. We all have one. Shit, I have several."

I rubbed the back of my neck, feeling the tension mounting. "But the difference is you didn't catch some chick fondling your boyfriend's cock."

Jade's lips pursed. "Uh...hello? Did you forget the Justin scandal? Nothing's more fucked up than discovering a selfie of your boyfriend going down on his mom's bestie."

We shuddered. It was an image we'd both wanted to burn from our memories.

I smirked. "Yeah, but you got even by sending the selfie to his parents and the woman's husband."

"Exactly. No one fucks with a Bellisario." She smiled smugly. "It was the biggest divorce scandal that summer." Only Jade could take heartbreak and turn it into a reality show.

"Well, I lost my chance to get revenge on Kyle years ago."

Jade tilted her head and stared at me incredulously. "Are you fucking kidding me? Look at you." She leaned forward and tapped Kirby on his shoulder. "Isn't she gorgeous?"

Kirby winked at me in the rearview mirror. "Absolutely."

"See?" Jade smiled like a Cheshire cat. "You're gorgeous, smart, talented, and still standing tough, like a damn warrior princess. Believe me, that's the greatest revenge against arrogant asswipes like Kyle Fillion. You didn't crumble and blow away like he'd hoped."

"Yeah, but it was real close."

Jade slapped my thigh. "Not on my damn watch."

She was right. I hadn't crumbled or blown away, but I had changed too much after what happened that night. I blinked back the pain, remembering the pivotal night that was still vivid in my mind.

That night had started out with so much happiness and excitement. I was practically giddy when Jade and I pulled up in the driveway of Kyle's parents' enormous redbrick mansion. I had pinched myself for being so lucky. I was Kyle's girlfriend. After months of me crushing on him hard, gorgeous Kyle had finally noticed me and smiled at me one day in chemistry class.

He'd taken my breath away. He was the hottest guy in my high school, and it hadn't hurt that his parents were New York City's most influential political couple. Kyle was destined for greatness. Everyone expected it.

We had come from different worlds, but he'd chosen me over all the girls clamoring for him. Those girls had come from the right families and looked the part—blond, lithe, and beautiful. But he hadn't seemed to care, and just like a tornado, he'd swept into my life and validated that I was worthy of love. He'd said all the right things, making me believe I was special, and in turn, I'd given him everything.

I thought we were in love, and I'd even lost my virginity to him, fucking him on his parents' boat on my birthday. That night had turned into Kyle and me fucking like rabbits every weekend. Jade told me not to trust him, but I'd said fuck it and ignored her. I thought he was the one, so he was worth it. I should have listened. All the shit he'd told me was so unoriginal.

I laughed bitterly, remembering how nervous and excited I had been when we headed inside Kyle's pre-graduation bash, the hottest party that night. I couldn't wait to celebrate with Kyle, and like a fool, I'd resolved to shed my fear and utter the words I hadn't said since the day my dad died—I love you. I'd expected to find Kyle holding court, surrounded by his preppy friends, but he wasn't around, so I'd gotten some liquid courage before I set out to find him in the maze of the huge mansion. Just like everything in my damn life, happiness turned to dust the moment I pushed open his bedroom door. Kyle's designer jeans were gathered around his ankles while his cock was being fondled by some chick with perfectly smooth, highlighted blond hair that fell across her shoulders like a gorgeous curtain.

I remembered how I'd just stood there shocked with my mouth gaping open as if it were some sort of mirage. I watched as the girl glided up from kneeling with too much sway in her narrow hips. When she'd given me a smug look before sauntering out of the bedroom, it felt like a dagger to the heart.

"Kyle? How could you do this to me?" I'd rasped with tears streaming unchecked down my cheeks. "I love you." My voice had hitched.

His face had turned into a mask of hate that shocked me to the very core.

"Love?" He'd huffed out an arctic laugh. "Sin, this isn't love. It never was, and it never will be."

I'd flinched, like a punch was launched to my gut. "If this isn't love, then tell me, what the hell is it?" I'd stared at him with narrowed eyes, feeling my heart ice over inch by inch.

"What do you want from me? I haven't promised you anything, Sin!" He'd sneered while unhurriedly buckling his belt.

"We've been dating for months!" I'd yelled.

His jaw tightened. "No, we've been *fucking* for months." He'd walked up and stared at me without a trace of emotion in his beautiful blue eyes. "Sin, I'm going away to college, and you're staying here to work for your mother. It would never work out between us."

He'd reached out to touch my hair, but I smacked his hand away.

He shrugged. "Take it for what it is. We're over."

I'd stood there, feeling stupid that I'd allowed myself to be weakened after my dad's death. I couldn't believe I'd let Kyle into my heart and body. I never would have let him in if I had known he would hurt me and leave me drowning in the deep end.

"Over?" I'd frozen like a deer in headlights, gasping for breath as I sank into the murky waters of an emotional abyss.

Then he'd gone for the ultimate emotional bitch slap.

"Let's keep it real, Sin. What we had was fun but temporary. You and I know there's no way in hell I could bring you home to my parents. You just don't fit into my world."

His parting words had burned, fueling my hate fire.

Everything had clicked into place that night. To people like Kyle, it was perfectly acceptable to fuck a girl like me in secret and then discard me like trash, like a whore.

Jade nudged me, interrupting my disturbing trip down memory lane. "Sin, I'm not saying to forget. I'm saying you need to heal and let that shit go."

Jade was right, but the truth cut like a knife. I couldn't let it go. No matter how hard I tried to distance myself from the past, it was still stuck to me like shit on the bottom of my stiletto. I tried to scrape it off, but the residue and stench remained.

And Kyle Fillion was that stench, the shit that had lingered. He'd sabotaged the chance for any man to break through the thick ice encasing my heart. Many had tried, and all had failed. I wouldn't—no, I couldn't—trust again, not after Kyle had trampled my heart and pride like it didn't mean a thing.

I stared through the window, watching the blur of city lights as Kirby darted in and out of Manhattan traffic. The past didn't matter. Love didn't matter. Perfect love didn't exist. It was a cliché. I understood good, hard, and sweaty no-commitment sex. No emotions were required.

I looked at Jade and winked. "Enough of this sappy stuff. I'm over that shit. Let's get to partying. It's time to turn it up and toast to the end of my dark past."

Kirby pulled up in front of the club and opened the car door. I shivered from the icy blast of air whirling around us as we stepped out of the car. Jade looked every inch the rich diva as she swathed herself in a huge white-and-gray fur coat, which she wore over the top of a tight leather minidress, leaving her long, tanned legs on display. Meanwhile, for a night out on the town, I rocked my own design, a black silk pantsuit and black bustier. It was sexy with a hard edge, and it was a direct reflection of who I was now.

Jade strutted past the crowd freezing their asses off queued behind the red velvet rope. Giving a bored stare to the intimidating bouncer standing atop a set of stairs holding a tablet, she held out her hand. He grunted and stamped it, and the crowd grumbled.

"What does it look like in there tonight?" Jade asked.

"A mixture," he responded.

Then he stamped my hand.

"This is bullshit. How come they don't have to wait in line?" a female in the line complained.

Shifting uncomfortably, I avoided the heated glares of the crowd. I still wasn't completely at ease with bypassing the line outside the club and going right in with VIP status. But Jade had clued me in on how the whole club thing worked. It was a silent business relationship. The clubs liked to pretty up their establishments, and the fact that Jade was rich and came from a famous family was a bonus. She would party at the club, and the club would comp her drinks. If she liked the place, she would invite her rich, beautiful friends, making that club the hottest place to be.

The bouncer stepped aside, and I followed Jade into the trendy New York City nightspot, located in the borough of Brooklyn, that edged a little closer toward bar-with-a-dance-floor territory. I loved this club. It was one of my favorite places to party. The whole scene felt fairly Miami-inspired with mojitos and drinks that came in real coconuts. The crowd was culturally diverse. The club would have DJ nights or live bands that rolled out sets chock-full of rock, salsa, merengue, samba, rumba, reggaeton, calypso, and a smattering of old-school hip-hop.

An eager hostess hurried over to us as we stepped over the threshold, ready to provide us with the VIP treatment. She escorted us to the lush lounge area with VIP seating where we could indulge in superior table service or just sit in the all-black mezzanine lounge.

Minutes later, Jade and I were sipping our drinks while watching some of the upscale crowd walk around like sheep in the same designer clothes. Their clothing was boring, with no originality, which was one of the main reasons I'd decided to move forward with my dream of designing my own clothing line. After losing the monotony battle with my closet, I knew I had to change the rules. If I couldn't find what I wanted to wear, I would make it instead.

Jade stared at me knowingly. "No thinking about business tonight."

She dragged me onto the dance floor. I closed my eyes, enjoying the exuberant energy of the salsa rhythm. My eyes snapped open when I felt a pair of hands wrap around my waist. "What the...?" I snapped before being spun around and finding Jaxon's blue eyes staring down at me.

God, he even smells good. Damn.

Jade smiled naughtily before sauntering away.

Jaxon leaned in, and his lips brushed against my ear. "When am I going to get your number?"

I rolled my eyes. "Uh...I don't give my number to stalkers." I swayed my body to the beat, enjoying the pressure of his hands on my hips a little too much.

"Stalker? Wow! I've never been called that before."

"Don't you think it's fitting for a guy who always ends up at the same club I'm at?"

This wasn't me making idle chitchat. It was a fact. In one way or another, Jaxon and I always seemed to end up at the same parties. Tonight was the first time I actually took the time to study his face. Blond and handsome, he was tall, that was for sure, and his toned, golden body told me he hadn't missed a session with his personal trainer. By his cocky smile, I knew he was all too aware of his good looks.

"Dance with me?" he asked, flashing his teeth, his voice low and sexy.

I arched a brow. "You know how to dance to salsa?"

"Of course," he said into my ear. "One dance."

The beat of the music thumped as he looked at me with a question in his eyes while his hands squeezed my hips.

I shrugged.

His hips pressed sensually against mine as he took my arms and placed them over his shoulders. He slid his hands along my back. Sighing, I allowed my body to caress his lean frame, my hips gyrating to the beat, and my body stirred.

Fuck it.

I grabbed a handful of his hair. It was soft to the touch, like silk running through my fingers. Pulling his face down, I ran my tongue against his lips just to test the chemistry, but when he tugged on my lower lip and kissed me hard, everything went from playful flirting to full-throttle fuck mode.

It wasn't long before my fingers were stroking through his hair as his fingers walked down my back and landed on my backside before squeezing my ass. I tilted my head back, looking at him through my lashes, before leaning forward, the tip of my tongue licking the heated skin of his throat.

The thoughts running through my mind were jumbled, irrational, and downright surprising. I wanted Jaxon more than my next breath. I nibbled and caressed the exposed skin, smiling when he shivered. The control I had over him was absolutely heady.

Jaxon growled as he picked me up and then pushed me against the wall of the club. To feel the desperation of his hands as they caressed me with an edge of trembling neediness was hot as freaking hell. His mouth touched and nipped me like he was a man on a mission. By the time I came up for air, my lips were swollen and my eyes were glazed over.

He didn't smile. In fact, his eyes were the most serious I'd ever seen.

"I could say a lot of pretty words right now, but they wouldn't mean shit. I want you." He slid me down to my feet. "Come home with me tonight."

I couldn't keep my hands off him. Spreading out my fingers across his back, I enjoyed the way the sensual heat of his skin seeped into my fingers.

He stared at me with unwavering focus. "Is that a yes?"

I nodded. "Yes," I whispered.

I could still taste him on my lips. I wanted to have this

moment, knowing it would all disappear in the morning. I would walk away then, never to see him again. And that made me want him even more.

Jaxon gestured toward the vigilant hostess who flittered through the club. She practically tripped over her feet trying to get over to him. "Sir?" she asked.

"Tell the valet to bring my car around," he said briskly before pulling me over to the lounge area where Jade was flirting outrageously with some guy.

I passed her my empty coconut and said bluntly, "I'm leaving."

"You treat her good." She stared coldly at Jaxon.

His face tightened. "Always."

Her eyes narrowed. "You better. I know exactly where to find you."

They glared at each other. I rolled my eyes. "Guys. You do realize I'm standing right here?" They stared at me blankly. "I can take care of myself."

"I'm just making sure Jaxon understands you're like family. No one fucks with my family." Jade winked at me. "Call Kirby when you're ready to go home, and he'll be there ASAP to get you."

I nodded before Jaxon and I pushed our way through the crowd, heading for the exit. As we walked out into the cold air, an expensive-looking silver car pulled up. The valet stepped out, handed the key to Jaxon, and then opened my door. After I slid in and sank down into the leather seat, we exchanged no words as we pulled away. When he put his hand on my thigh with the promise of things to come, I shoved it away. I wasn't big on intimate touching.

He frowned. "You okay?"

"Yeah." I smiled slightly. "Just didn't think tonight would end with me going home with you."

He smirked. "Don't worry. I'll still respect you in the morning."

I laughed. "The question is, will I still respect you?"

He looked at me, his eyes traveling over my body. "I guess that depends on how I perform, huh?"

"Pretty much."

He pulled up in front of a building I recognized from multiple photos in magazines. It was where many celebrities lived. He swerved his car into the underground parking garage before pulling into a space. He turned off the ignition, and I waited for him to come around and open my door.

Then he said, "Look, I don't want you to think I'm running a game on you, but I have to say, I've been watching you for a long time."

I smirked. "All confirming my initial stalker assessment."

He gripped the steering wheel and then released it. "Sin, you're not like all the other women I know."

I rolled my eyes. "You mean rich, spoiled, and boring?"

"No. I mean beautiful, independent, and inaccessible." He paused. "I just don't want you to think this is all about me fucking you."

Oh God!

I was going to lose my shit if he started spewing some crazy promise, thinking it would make what we were about to do seem more romantic. I wasn't looking for romance. It didn't fucking exist—at least, not in my world.

"Jaxon, you don't have to promise me anything. In fact, I would prefer if you didn't because I can't give you anything beyond tonight."

"What if I want more than tonight?" His eyes hardened.

I pulled out my cell. "Then I need to call my ride because I can't give that to you."

He placed his hand over mine and squeezed. "I'll take tonight."

He leaned in and kissed me, but I hesitated. Something just felt...wrong. It was almost as if shackles were being slapped around my wrists. I pulled back, but he pressed forward, his tongue coaxing mine.

I broke off the kiss, but he was not deterred.

He nuzzled his face into my hair and then backed away. "Ready?" he asked.

I stared at him. "Tonight only." I wanted to be perfectly clear that's all he would get.

"I hear you, Sin." He ran a finger across my cheek before getting out of the car.

There was something about his response and his blank stare that made me pause. Common sense battled with the heat between my legs, and the shameless need to have sex with Jaxon won.

As we stepped into the elevator, Jaxon grabbed my hand, but I pulled it away. There would be no bonding or cuddle time or whispers of sweet nothings.

This was all about straight-up sex.

Jaxon placed a guiding hand on my back as we walked toward his door, and I tried to calm my uneasiness. Jade was right. Maybe I was too paranoid. Maybe I did overthink things way too much. *Jaxon is cool. He knows this is only a sex proposition.*

I took a calming breath as I strode over the threshold. I stared at all the expensive furniture. The apartment was freaking immaculate.

"This is new—a guy with a spotless apartment."

"Smoke and mirrors." He winked at me. "My mother pays for a cleaning service. She hates my messy habits."

His admission wasn't surprising and only confirmed my initial assessment. He was a spoiled mama's boy.

"That's interesting." I walked around, admiring the beautiful artwork and photos.

As I'd suspected, his parents were blond and beautiful just like him.

My body stiffened when I felt his arms wrap around me

possessively. He pulled me around and into him. I forced myself to relax as his lips came crashing down onto mine. I kissed him back eagerly, my tongue entering his mouth and exploring it fervently.

He lowered his hands from my back to my ass. He groaned as he cupped my ass cheeks, pushing me against his erection. "Playtime is over," he growled.

Taking my hand, he pulled me behind him until we were in his bedroom. I didn't resist when he gently pushed me onto the bed, his eyes focused on mine. I was used to this game of seduction. It all ended the same way, with my sexual itch scratched until fulfilled. I stared at him, enjoying the strip show, as he tugged off his black T-shirt, displaying his six-pack. His well-built body looked like he'd spent hours at the gym getting hard and gorgeous.

I started to take off my clothes when he grasped my hand.

"No, let me." He hauled me up and took off my jacket and top. His fingers expertly unhooked my bra before throwing it across the room. "Gorgeous," he mumbled. His eyes were dark and intense as he pressed me back onto the bed. His lips ravaged me as his hands undid my pants.

I lay there in my panties, wanting him more than ever. I shivered as his fingers pulled off my panties before slipping into my pussy and rubbing sensually against my wetness.

"I'll make this good for you, Sin. It'll be so good you'll never want to leave me."

That was where he was wrong. I would leave him in a heartbeat.

Jaxon leaped from the bed and ripped off his jeans along with his black underwear. I reached up and worked my fingers over his rock-hard cock, enjoying my power when he hissed with pleasure.

"Not yet, Sin." He pressed me against the bed before kissing me like a man on the verge of going full fuck mode on me.

I pushed his chest. "Condom," I whispered. "Where's the condom?"

He gave me a perplexed stare. "You're not on the pill?"

I snorted. "Even if I were, I wouldn't sleep with you without a condom. I'm STD-free, and I plan on staying that way."

His body stiffened. "What kind of guy do you think I am?"

I leaned up onto my elbows. "Hopefully, you're a guy who knows that fucking around without protection is fucking stupid."

He narrowed his eyes. "I don't have any STDs, Sin."

I looked at him incredulously. "Uh...that's good to know. Now, where's the condom?"

I sighed with relief when he slid off the bed and opened the drawer of his nightstand. He pulled out a big box of condoms.

I glared. *What the fuck? He has condoms, so why the hell was he making such a big deal about wearing one with me?*

"Now, wasn't that easy?" I asked him.

He rolled onto the bed and kissed me hard. "You're such a smartass."

"I just keep it real, rocker boy."

He stared at me, and I boldly glared right back. In the past, I would have been self-conscious of my curvy, toned body, but months ago, I'd accepted the woman I was. I was perfectly fine with how I looked, and from the hardness of his cock, so was he.

His head fell to my breasts, and his tongue darted out, circling one tight bud. I jerked at the hot, sensual slide of his tongue. Jaxon trailed his big hand across my stomach, pinning me to the bed, while he alternated between my nipples, licking and sucking each one.

"Jaxon, stop being such a fucking tease," I groaned as my hands reached up and tugged on his hair.

Ignoring me, he slipped his fingers into my damp folds. Moaning, I arched up, wiggling to get closer. His thumb circled and played with my clit as his wicked tongue wreaked havoc on my nipples until both turned to hard points.

Jaxon growled while yanking me higher onto the bed. Draping my knees over his shoulders, he dived face first into my pussy. His thick tongue flicked and lapped my clit with such savageness that I went over the edge, screaming his name like a prayer before I knew it.

Pulling back, he stared at me with satisfaction, with me glistening all over his mouth. "Again, Sin."

He pushed his fingers into me. I panted, my hair sweaty and tangled, as my hips gyrated.

"Scream for me again, Sin. I need to hear it. I need to know you crave me as much as I crave you."

He thrust his fingers harder and deeper. My back bucked, and I screamed like a madwoman. My toes curled as his fingers fucked me into another orgasm. By the time I came down from my sexually induced euphoria, Jaxon was right above me. He ripped open the packet and quickly slid the condom over his cock before lowering himself down onto me.

I groaned, wrapping my legs around him. My body hummed with anticipation. I felt the tip of his cock nudge my entrance before he finally slammed in. He moved his hands to either side of my shoulders as he looked down at me with possession stamped all over his face.

"Oh God, yes. Finally..." He groaned as he started to move slowly.

His cock was driving me insane. Thank God the rumors had been right. He did know how to fuck like a damn champion.

"Fuck me, Jaxon," I cried out.

He continued to piston in and out smoothly, his balls bumping against my ass. My eyes closed as the heat blossomed within my center. He pulled out and drilled back in, and with each thrust, he hit the right spot. I scraped my nails across his back as our bodies moved in perfect synchrony.

"No one but me," he said, pushing in farther.

My eyes popped open. "What?"

"No one else but me," he chanted.

He pulled out and sank back in, hitting my G-spot with every thrust.

Lost in my sex-crazed moment, I gasped out, "Fuck me harder!"

"I'll never let go," he growled as he lost control, pounding into me again and again.

My breathing hitched as my body shuddered, nearing explosion. His body convulsed as he roared. I climaxed with an intensity I had never experienced in my life.

Rolling over, he withdrew his cock from me and stared at me with a sexy, lazy smile. "Again. This time, you're on top," he demanded. He slipped the condom off and slid another one onto his still-hard cock.

I lay still, trying to get my breath back as I planned my graceful escape.

He pressed his lips against mine. "Stay, Sin." He nuzzled my neck. "Ride me."

I heard the neediness in his voice, and I hesitated. I couldn't decide whether I should follow my instincts and leave or give Jaxon a chance by pushing my past behind me. My gut clenched as I made a decision that countered anything I'd done in a while.

I swung my leg over his body and smiled. "My pleasure. If there's anything I adore, it's a good, hard ride."

❦ 3 ❦

SINTHIA

LEAVING TABITHA'S BOUTIQUE, I plowed my way through the chaotic evening crush of New Yorkers rushing to get home. I was exhausted. It had been a really long day, and my mind was still a damn cobweb of random thoughts. One in particular had me reeling.

He loves me? Holy shit!

A week later, I still couldn't believe it. Right in the middle of our early morning, hot-and-heavy fuck session, Jaxon had looked down at me with those gorgeous baby blues and blurted out that he loved me.

He loves me? Is he out of his damn mind?

We'd only hooked up one time. At first, I'd thought I was just hearing things when he said he loved me, but when he'd followed it up by saying he couldn't picture being with anyone but me, I freaked the hell out. I'd scrambled off the bed and pulled on my clothes like hellhounds were nipping at my heels.

I hadn't even called Kirby to pick me up. I'd rushed out of Jaxon's apartment so fast that I didn't remember to grab my favorite designer underwear. When I'd gotten back to Jade's penthouse, I realized I was fucking commando. *Shit!* And I loved those see-through pink panties. I'd stalked them for months until they finally went on sale.

I shook my head. *I need a cup of coffee.*

My cell rang. *Restricted* with no phone number came up on the caller ID, but I answered, knowing what would happen. The person would hang up immediately or hold on for a few seconds to listen to my irate cursing before hanging up. It had been happening for days, and it was fucking maddening.

I shoved my cell into my handbag and kept walking farther into the quiet part of town. The streets were blissfully empty—no traffic and no rude pedestrians pushing and shoving one another. First, I needed coffee, and then I was going straight home to sketch clothing designs.

I stopped at the corner and waited for a taxi to pass before I crossed the street. Halfway across, I nearly swallowed my tongue when a dark car sped out of the darkness, barreling toward me. In the nick of time, I jumped back onto the sidewalk and watched in horror as the car sideswiped a parked one and then kept going.

What the fuck?

Shaken, I stood frozen. My heart raced.

Oh God, is someone trying to kill me?

Stop it, Sin. You're just being paranoid.

I straightened my jacket and started to cross the street again, only to snap my head to my left when that same dark car peeled around the corner with its headlights off. It screeched to a stop three cars away from where I stood frozen with one foot on the curb and the other in the street. The driver revved the engine menacingly. I gritted my teeth, stepping fully into the street to square off with the car, trying to see who was inside, but the tinted windows prevented me from seeing the driver's face.

Fuck this.

I wasn't going to let some crazy person scare me. I started walking toward the car. The driver revved the engine again and then sped toward me.

Oh, hell no!

I hopped back onto the sidewalk, running in the opposite direction, picking up full speed when I heard the roar of the engine. I looked back, and oddly, it had stopped. My heart leaped into my throat. Not hesitating, I turned back around and ran so hard my chest burned from the effort.

I didn't stop running until I got to Jade's building, bypassing the doorman who was talking to a police officer. Huffing and puffing, I stepped into the elevator. I grabbed my knees, trying to catch my breath. The whole ride up, two thoughts raced through my mind—one, *Damn! I need to get in fucking shape*, and two, *Someone is definitely stalking me.*

Walking out of the elevator, I felt my pulse quicken at the sight of Jade's neighbors standing and talking in the hallway. When a police officer came out of the penthouse, I ran in with dread pooling in my stomach. I skidded to a stop when I saw Jade looking around the apartment with a frown.

"What the hell happened?" I croaked.

"The strangest shit ever," she responded, gesturing toward the door. "When I got home, the door was wide open. I know I locked it. I panicked. All I could think about was that all our shit had been stolen."

I looked around. "What was stolen?"

She frowned. "Not a damn thing. That's the strange part. I looked around, and nothing was gone or out of place. I called the police just in case. This type of shit doesn't happen in this neighborhood—let alone this building." She strolled over to the refrigerator and pulled out two bottles of water.

Thirsty, I walked over, grabbed one, and drank it. Pulling my hair away from my face, I grimaced at the dampness on my forehead from the sweat. "What about the security cameras?"

She shrugged. "I checked with security. There's nothing on them." She stared at me. "This is a new look for you. What's going on with the grimy, flustered thing you have happening?"

"Some fucker tried to run me the hell down," I mumbled before taking a large gulp.

Jade choked on her water. "What?"

"Long story, but I think someone is trying to frighten me or, worst-case scenario, kill me." I nibbled on my bottom lip.

Jade came over and hugged me before stepping back. "Are you sure it wasn't just some crazy New York driver?"

"Oh, I'm sure. New York drivers tend to leave the scene of an accident. They don't come back. This car did and fucking terrorized me for blocks." I leaned my hip against the granite counter.

"I don't like this," Jade said.

"You think?" I asked tiredly.

Way too many strange things had happened over the span of a couple of days, and I didn't believe in coincidences.

Jade's eyes clouded over with worry. "I decided to change the locks, and the locksmith should be here shortly. You go take a hot bath and relax. I can wait on my own. You have an early morning."

"Yeah, that's what I need. My nerves are fried right about now." I couldn't even think about working on my sketches.

Walking through the apartment, I started peeling off my jacket. My mind unfocused, I didn't even realize I was in my bedroom until I stepped over the threshold. As I threw my jacket onto the bed, I nearly fainted when I saw something unthinkable lying there. The pair of pink panties I'd left at Jaxon's apartment were wrapped around a long-stemmed white rose.

Just like I'd thought, there was no such thing as a coincidence.

4

SINTHIA

SEVEN YEARS LATER...PRESENT DAY

I LOVED SUMMER NIGHTS IN MANHATTAN. SULTRINESS lingered in the air as New Yorkers hustled to their Friday night of fun. *But damn, it is hot.* Now I was cursing my decision to walk instead of catching a cab to the club.

I pulled my auburn hair away from my neck. Every muscle in my body was fatigued from working all day on my new fashion collection. My body begged for me to slow down, but my mind raced a mile a minute with lists of things I hadn't completed.

Maybe I bit off more than I can chew. Just the thought made me queasy.

This collection would make me or break me. It was a scary reality, but it was my reality.

When Lily Sanchez, an energetic buyer from a Fifth Avenue luxury goods department store, had walked into my friend Francisco "Cisco" Rodriguez's upscale boutique and fallen instantly in love with my couture clothing that he sold in his store, she'd changed my life forever. Just like that, at twenty-six years old, I'd moved from fledgling darling of the fashion world to having several luxury goods buyers clamoring to carry my edgy Sin Michaels women's wear line in their stores.

Expanding from selling in posh boutiques, including Tabitha's and Cisco's, to going full throttle in department stores was a scary proposition. Frankly, I was comfortable with selling my clothing in small venues and making a name for myself with my signature street-smart style.

But Lily was right. Being *comfortable* wasn't enough anymore. It was time for me to expand, and I was ready—well, almost ready. I needed financing to help me manufacture my new line, or my dream would die. I was slowly digging myself out of a ton of debt, so no bank would ever give me a loan. So I had been floored and excited when Tabitha called me. She'd been practically giddy that one of her business connections would provide financing in exchange for a small percentage of my future profits. The ink hadn't even dried on the business contract when two million dollars was deposited into my business account with the promise of another million in six months.

Can I really make my new line a reality?

I took a deep, cleansing breath, refusing to go down the destructive path of self-doubt. This was a very exciting time in my life. I should be jumping up and down at the lucky turn of events that had changed my life for the better. But instead, I was focused on all the things that could turn it to dust.

I was finally standing outside the nondescript warehouse. It was a tricky place to find on a little street with minimal signage.

Shit, if it weren't for the big, beefy man positioned in front of the entrance, I would have bypassed it completely.

With interest, I watched as a couple practically pawed at each other while strolling up to the bouncer, who promptly turned them away. Frowning, I strutted up to the burly guy blocking the club's entrance.

"Sin Michaels," I said while simultaneously handing him my ID.

He scanned my ID through a device attached to his tablet. He smiled as his eyes focused on my ample breasts.

I snapped my fingers. "Hey! Up here."

He leered in a simply icky way that said he didn't give a shit before glancing down at his tablet. "The rest of your party isn't here yet, but you can go in." He gestured toward my wrist and then placed a black-and-gold wristband around it.

I arched a brow.

He winked. "It lets the guests know you're not interested in playing. As hot as you are, sweetness, you're going to need it just to keep them off you." He stepped aside. "Welcome to the McKay Club."

I snorted. He'd said *the McKay Club* like it was a religious shrine. Everyone knew about the McKay Club. It was part of a chain of private clubs owned by the wealthy New York City recluse and business mogul, Core McKay. According to insiders, all his clubs were invite-only playgrounds for the elite, rich, and kinky to indulge in discreet liaisons, allowing all their freaky fantasies to come true.

Why the fuck would anyone want to have a business meeting in a fetish club?

The rhythm of the music slammed into my body like a sledgehammer as I stepped over the threshold. Each thump felt like a nail sinking into my head, awakening the migraine I was fighting to suppress. All I wanted to do was go home, put on my comfy yoga pants, and pass out from sheer exhaustion.

Scanning the dark corners of the room, I noticed McKay's looked more like a lavish penthouse than a club. The decor was strangely sensual and intimate, with Asian motifs, bamboo screens, and paintings dotting the walls throughout.

My gaze wandered to the bouncer standing guard before an entrance draped with expensive-looking fabric. He stepped aside, giving way to the men and women flashing their ink-black wristbands. It was probably a room where all the off-the-wall sexual debauchery happened. I was so not interested in going inside.

I sighed, deliberately walking up to the bouncer blocking the entrance. He pointed to my wristband. "Sorry. This area is invite only."

I scoffed. "I don't—"

My tirade was interrupted by a tap on my shoulder. Annoyed, I looked over my shoulder, almost biting my tongue when I locked eyes with a gorgeous man staring at me with more than a little interest.

"Are you going in?" he asked in a smooth, baritone voice.

"What?" I croaked before clearing my throat. "No. I'm not."

"Well, that's a shame." He winked at me before showing the bouncer his wrist and pushing aside the fabric. He strode through without a second glance. Curious, I tried to get a glimpse of the area through the slit of the closing curtain.

The bouncer rudely snapped it shut. "Like I said, invite only."

Pursing my lips, I asked, "How do I get to the rooftop bar?"

He pointed over to the discreetly placed elevator, and I made a beeline for it. The trip up to the roof took mere seconds, and the doors slid open to reveal women carrying high-end purses and lots of men in suits and ties. I could almost smell the money wafting through the air. Just when I thought the rooftop was the PG version of downstairs, I saw the semi-nude bodies gyrating and reenacting scenes from a porn movie on the dance floor.

Inching through the crowd, I made my way toward the bar. I just wanted to get this business meeting over with and leave. Ignoring the interested stares from men and women who were more focused on my legs than their drinks, I reached my objective.

I beckoned the bartender, requesting a dry gin martini.

He nodded and walked away.

I scoffed at the smoldering gaze of a pretty boy who looked

like he'd stepped out of a fashion magazine. His hair was too perfectly styled, and his clothing had come straight off the runway. I rolled my eyes when he stopped in front of me, smiling with bleached teeth that nearly blinded me. He wasn't remotely close to my type—too sweet-looking. I liked my men hard and edgy, with tattoos decorating every inch of their exposed, muscled bodies.

He glanced down at my bracelet and then up to my breasts, like he wanted to ask them out on a date. "Hello."

I frowned. *Pretty boy was aiming too high.*

Holding up my hand in his face, I said, "No. Just no. Okay?"

Thankfully, he shrugged before walking away, probably deciding I wasn't worth the effort or the embarrassment.

The bartender slid the martini between my fingers. After picking up the glass, I sipped the drink as I watched Tabitha sway toward me, looking as gorgeous as ever in a head-to-toe black ensemble that accented her sensuous body. Beside Jade, Tabitha was my favorite person. She was a talented designer and my mentor. Behind her polished veneer of Tabitha Thorp, celebrity designer, only I knew that she had grown up on the rough streets of Brooklyn, *doing things she wasn't really proud of—* her words, not mine. I wanted to know what those things were, but she wouldn't share the gossip about that part of her life, so I'd just left it alone.

"Hey, Tabi! I can't stop drooling over your outfit," I said cheekily.

Tabitha kissed me on my cheek. "That's precious. The designer is salivating over her own design." She nudged me with her elbow. "Yes, oh, queen of fashion, you are so great. Let's all dance around and bask in your creative hotness."

I smiled. "Okay, yes, I was fishing for compliments. You don't have to rub it in."

Tabitha eyed me. "What the hell are you wearing?"

I batted my eyes innocently. "Huh?"

"You lied. You said it wasn't finished. I want it. Take it off now."

"You like?" I looked at her coyly. "I'm bringing booty back." I nodded toward the crowded dance floor. "Go run and tell them skinny bitches."

The black leather dress was super short in the front and longer in the back, flaring out around my curvy hips. The skintight corset pushed up my ample breasts while cinching my narrow waist.

"I just finished it today, and I wanted to take it for a twirl—you know, show the people what I'm working with." I smiled saucily.

This was my freak-'em dress, and from the way the men's eyes were following me, I hadn't lost it. More importantly, once I added it to my collection, it would fly off the rack.

Tabitha's smirk disappeared. I knew she spotted the shadows under my eyes.

"Sin, you're working too hard. You need to take a break, have a bit of relaxation. How about that vacation you said you and Jade were going on?"

I rolled my eyes. "Any vacation with Jade wouldn't be relaxation. It would be a nonstop party, and I don't have the strength for that right now. Besides, I have a whole collection to design."

Tabitha's pouty lips pursed. "You have to rest, Sin. You're driving yourself into the ground."

My face tightened. "Well, that's cute—advice coming from the president of the workaholic club. No thanks. I have a lot of work to do. Speaking of work, I left early to attend this meeting." I pressed forward. "So, where's my investor?" My lips pursed with displeasure.

I really hated the word *investor*. It was too mysterious, and not in a good way. Knowing the rough crowd she did business with, it was damn near sinister.

"He just called me. He can't make it. He has a business deal to wrap up, but his partner, Ram Steele, will be coming in his place."

I glowered. "He called an emergency meeting and then doesn't show? Sounds like some bullshit to me."

Tabitha shrugged. "He's a very busy man."

Staring at her like she'd lost her mind, I responded, "And I'm not? What's with all this mystery?" I hissed. "Why can't I know his damn name?"

Tabitha's eyes hardened. "Darling, the less you know, the better. Believe me."

My hands tightened around the glass stem. *Shit! That's exactly what I'm afraid of.*

"Sin, I swear to you he's legit. I wouldn't get you involved if he weren't."

I stared at her with disapproval.

Tabitha sighed heavily. "Sin, you can't have it both ways. You asked me to find an investor, and I did. You got the money. Isn't that all that matters now?"

Is it?

Frankly, I didn't know, but what I did know was that I wouldn't be able to complete my collection without this mysterious investor.

My body slowly relaxed. "You're right." I sighed heavily while tapping my fingers against the glass. "I guess I'm anxious about why he wanted to meet me. Shit, it's been several months since he gave me the money, and he hasn't met me once. Why does he want to meet now?" My eyes widened. "Is he concerned about my business being able to make a profit?"

Tabitha shrugged. "Don't know. I didn't ask."

I arched a brow. "You didn't ask?"

"He's not exactly the type of man you question. He orders, and you do it. That's it."

I furrowed my brows with concern. "Oh God." I gulped my drink.

He was a control freak. This was going to be a mess if he wanted to step in now and micromanage the way I ran my business.

Squished by the mounting crowd, Tabitha bumped me with her elbow and hip. I instantly adjusted to make room for her to lean against the bar.

"Look, there's nothing to worry about." She glanced around curiously. "He's pretty much hands-off until he thinks the business isn't going to make a profit. And your business is on the cusp of making a shitload of money. If it weren't, believe me, he wouldn't have given you the money in the first place." She paused. "Be grateful, Sin. It could be worse. My investor is up my ass on every collection. Do you know what that does to the creative process?" She wrapped a hand around my waist and gently squeezed. "Sin, will you relax? Why can't you just enjoy your success without adding drama?"

Nothing about my life had been easy, especially since I'd walked away from my mother, Grace. I'd had to fight, scratch, and crawl to get to where I was today. I knew I'd earned the right to be here, but I couldn't help looking over my shoulder, waiting for the bubble to burst.

I took a calming breath. "God, you're right. I'm worrying for nothing."

Tabitha winked at me. "That's right, baby. Now let's order a round of martinis, toast to the good life, and hope Mr. Steele drags his ass here sooner rather than later, before we both get pissy drunk."

She gestured for the bartender, but he was already heading toward us with two dry gin martinis.

"Dry gin martinis," he said, sliding a drink each toward Tabitha and me.

"We didn't order drinks," I said, tapping my fingers against the bar.

He smiled beautifully. "Courtesy of the gentleman." He nodded toward a dark-haired man leaning against the bar.

His muscles bunching against his crisp white tailored shirt, it was hard not to notice the tall man staring at me. Tilting my head, I glared boldly at him. Even in the room full of gorgeous men, he didn't blend in with the crowd. He was hot—well, hot and scary. He didn't even smile. In fact, he was scowling at me with menace pouring from him like a dark cloud.

Tabitha's doe eyes widened before she cleared her throat. "Well, isn't he yummy?" she growled, looking sideways at me with a smirk. "So are you going to go over there and thank him?"

He looked like trouble waiting to fucking happen. I lifted the martini glass to my lips, continuing to stare at my new sinful fixation.

"Nope. Just like at the zoo, I like to gawk at dangerous and beautiful creatures from afar."

She jabbed me in the side. "For fuck's sake, you're licking the rim of your glass while eye-fucking him."

Shit! My tongue stopped mid-twirl. I hadn't even realized I'd been doing it. *Damn it!*

I scowled at her before draining my glass. I should be at home, sleeping. Instead, I was leering at some man like I was a sex-starved freak. I snatched the drink he'd sent.

"Jesus, what the hell am I doing here?" I mumbled under my breath.

Tabitha hip checked me, wiggling her body to the thumping beat of the music. "It's okay to break out of your vanilla world and walk on the wild side." She raised her eyebrows.

"Uh-huh." I sighed. "Absolutely not. He's off-limits," I responded flatly.

He was gorgeous, just plain fucking gorgeous. His dark hair was shaved short. His searing gray eyes made me seriously horny. His stark features blended well with his chiseled cheekbones and painfully hard jaw. His body was pure rippling muscle, but he was completely not my type. He looked like CEO material, and I was damn sure I wasn't remotely close to his type of woman, especially with my nontraditional clothing and tattoo-covered back.

I deliberately turned and pulled my long auburn hair over my shoulder, giving him a full view of the intricate tattoos covering my back. I was hoping he would just move on to the Barbielooking women eyeing him with lustful eyes. I looked over my shoulder smugly, but he was still standing there, staring at me.

Shit. Well, this is new.

Running my hands through my hair with trembling fingers, I mumbled, "Tell me again. Why am I doing this shit? I've got a ton of work to do."

Tabitha rolled her eyes. "Like what?"

"I have clients depending on me."

Tabitha choked on her martini. "Sin, you're a clothing designer not a doctor. Besides, you haven't had a date in months. You work nonstop. Just enjoy the interest of a sexy man."

Feeling his scorching gaze, I turned and stared at him. His eyes flashed as he arched his eyebrow at me. There was no smile. It was probably something he didn't know how to do. When he crossed his muscular arms, my eyes traveled up his tall, well-built body, stopping at his piercing, bright gray eyes. My fingers clenched, wanting so badly to run through his blunt-cut, midnight-black hair.

Shit, shit, shit.

It was going to be another long night of pushing Beast, my favorite vibrator, to the breaking point.

Breaking eye contact with the man, I looked over at Tabitha. "I need to stop. I don't want to raise his expectations because I'm damn sure not taking him home tonight." I nudged her. "Why don't you go over and tame him?"

Tabitha pouted playfully. "Well, unfortunately, the gorgeous lion isn't into me. If he were, I would be over there in a heartbeat, ready and willing to take him down as if I were on a safari."

I laughed, nearly choking on my drink. "I've never had a man stare at me with such intensity. It's like I'm a deer he wants to chase down and eat. Don't get me wrong. I'm not opposed to being eaten by a good-looking man." I waggled my eyebrows.

Tabitha swatted me playfully. "You're so naughty, and I love it."

"But what's up with the I-want-to-rip-you-apart stare?"

"Well, go find out," she responded dryly, gently prodding me forward.

I shot her an annoyed scowl, rooting myself to the spot. "Hell to the no."

Tabitha groaned. "What happened to fun Sin?"

I grinned. "She sharpened her his-dick-ain't-worth-the-trouble detector. With this guy, my detector is ringing like a motherfucker." I winked at her. "Beep, beep, beep."

Tabitha laughed. "Girl, you're a hot mess." Her cell rang. "About time. That's Ram calling. I have to go somewhere quiet to hear. I'll be right back." She started to walk off, and then she stopped. "And when I come back, I want all the juicy details on the lion. Now, scoot." She waved good-bye before walking away with her cell pressed to her ear.

I turned and stared at him. His eyebrow lifted, and my own answered.

"Oh, fuck it."

I strode toward him, and as I stopped in front of him, I tossed my long hair over my shoulder while I licked my bottom lip. Awareness strummed through me. I planted my feet firmly, gathering my strength around me until the menace shrouding him like a veil ceased to intimidate me. I forced my gaze to linger over him, and then my eye caught sight of it—the all-seeing eye tattoo on the side of his neck.

Sweet baby Jesus. I'm in big fucking trouble.

"What do you want?" I asked.

Our eyes locked. The power of his demanding stare willed me to lower my eyes, but I forced myself not to do that. His eyebrow lifted, and mine furrowed. His eyes traveled from the top of my head down to my curvy body, seeming to like every-thing about it. I swallowed hard, trying hard not to squirm under his sensuous stare. He lifted his glass to his crazy-sexy hot lips and sipped his drink. My breasts tingled, and my nipples went rock hard.

Jesus, who the fuck is this man?

"The question is, do you know what you want?" he rasped with his eyes flickering in the twinkling city lights.

Holy shit!

I had to squeeze my thighs together as my sex clenched with need. His face twitched. I pinched back the urge to caress the light jagged scar running across his eyebrow.

"Does that line normally work on women?" I rolled my eyes.

Humor flashed in his eyes, but then it faded, and his gray eyes glinted. For a long couple of minutes, we just stared at each other.

"You tell me." His voice was diamond-hard.

Uncertainty crept up on me. "Can't confirm or deny." I inclined my head, refusing to cower.

He assessed me with his eyes as I waited for him to say something.

"This is not a battle, darling."

His deep drawl had my heart instantly pounding while goose bumps formed along my arms. His magnetism intrigued me, much to my annoyance.

"If it were, you wouldn't have a chance in hell of winning," he said without a trace of warmth reflecting in his cold eyes.

Something about this man made me rise to his unspoken challenge.

"I beg to differ. I tend to fight dirty."

His eyes flashed. There was no humor, just raw steel. Awareness hummed through me.

"We're not fighting, so you can relax. I just saw a beautiful woman and bought her a drink."

His low, gravelly voice strummed over my body, and a vision of him whispering very kinky shit while fucking me flashed through my mind.

Shit!

I couldn't look away from this arrogant ass. My creative streak wouldn't allow it. He was a work of art. He wasn't classically handsome or a pretty boy. He was very attractive in a rugged and dangerous way. He had eyes the color of steel, and I was fascinated by the way he watched me, like he could read my mind and knew exactly what I was thinking. And I was thinking of all sorts of filthy, dirty things that I'd bet he was well versed in doing.

"Is this your first time here at McKay?" One of his dark eyebrows cocked.

I squirmed from the dampness in my panties. "First and last." I ignored my arousal and focused on him.

"Not your type of crowd?" The corner of his mouth twitched with suppressed amusement, but it was gone as soon as it had arrived.

"I don't do kink clubs. I like my sexual exploits to be a little more private," I retorted.

He leaned down and whispered in my ear, "You have no idea what you're missing, darling."

My mouth parted at his words. My pussy clenched so hard my knees almost buckled. This wasn't good. This was going way past the normal snarky-flirt-then-walk-away routine. Something about him intrigued me, and I couldn't figure out what it was.

"Fuck," I blurted, fighting the crazy impulse to lay myself at his feet.

He lifted his damn beautiful brow again, and I forced myself not to freak out from the pure sexiness of this man.

A small smile played on his lips. "Is that an invitation, darling?" He lifted my hand before I could stop him, and then he brushed his hard lips against the backs of my fingers. "Because I'm more than happy to accept."

When I felt the nip of his teeth against my skin, my breathing became shallow and erratic. I quickly pulled my hand back. "It wasn't an invitation. It was a statement." I held up my mostly empty glass to my lips and tilted it, draining the contents for liquid courage. I was horrified and disgusted that my body was responding to this cocky bastard.

He stared at me like a cat playing with a mouse. "Let me get you another."

My heart jumped in panic. "No, not interested," I hastened to say. "Look…" I arched a brow, waiting for his name.

He arched a brow right back.

"Okay…so you buy me a drink but refuse to give me your name?"

He stepped closer. He was so close I could smell the tantalizing fragrance notes of sandalwood, cedar, and rich amber from the cologne he wore. His hand lightly touched my hip, like he was branding me as his possession. I should have moved away, but frankly, I couldn't. My mind was telling me to get my shit together, but my body rebelled and became even more aroused.

"My name is meaningless since you're too afraid to explore anything beyond this drink." As he leaned over, his lips deliberately brushed my lobe while he whispered in my ear, "Such a shame. I was just starting to have fun."

He pulled back and gave me a sly, dark stare that licked my skin, setting me afire. His arrogance should have been irritating, but all I could think was, *How would his callused fingers feel on my bare skin?* Curiosity added to my inner struggle.

"So I guess that makes you the big, bad wolf in this club," I stated flatly.

He shrugged. "No, I'm just a man who recognizes a woman who's bored with men dropping at her knees." He cocked his head. "Your mind and body crave a challenge. You want to know what it would feel like to drop to your knees before a man." He raised his eyebrow. "Do you want to take a walk on the wild side, darling?"

Mesmerized, I watched his hand reach out.

His callused finger slid across my cheek. "Do you want to play with the big, bad wolf?"

My eyelids fluttered at his words. I could almost imagine myself kneeling between his thighs with his huge hands wrapped around the back of my head. I swallowed hard, snapping back from the edge of insanity. This man was definitely a do-not-touch situation. Pulling away, I was determined to put some distance between us.

"I'm not interested." The words tumbled out of my mouth.

He stroked his index finger over my bottom lip. "There is no strength in denial, darling."

My mouth fell open, and then my tongue flicked over the pad of his finger, tasting a hint of scotch and cigar.

"Good girl," he said lazily, watching me with a heavy-lidded gaze.

Fear spiked. *Sweet Jesus, this man makes me want to lower myself at his feet.*

That would defy everything I was—strong, powerful, and in charge. I snapped my head back, and my lips snapped shut, but he caught me firmly by the jaw.

"Calm yourself. Don't run from what your mind and body know you need." He clamped his fingers onto my chin, gently stroking as if he were calming a baby. The peacefulness of his touch contradicted the iciness in his eyes.

My thoughts spiraled. I cleared my throat and swallowed hard. "Get your hand off my face."

It annoyed me that he touched me so casually, so possessively. There was no asking for fucking permission. He acted like I actually belonged to him.

His slightly mocking smile returned, and he dropped his hand from my face. I knew he'd let go because he wanted to, not because I'd demanded. This man was like no man I'd ever encountered. He brought out a submissive side I hadn't been aware I had, but I had no intention of ever exploring. I needed to leave. Playtime was over, and I was grabbing my toys and going home—alone.

"Well, this was entertaining, but I'll pass on the bullshit you're shoveling."

He took my hand with a domineering gleam in his eyes. My

breath caught as I felt the slide of warm liquid between my thighs.

"I'll see you again, darling." He caressed my palm with his fingers, revving the scorching connection between our bodies.

My clit throbbed with greediness. His mesmerizing touch stoked the flames of awareness, holding me captive. The dark, sensual promise in his eyes chilled me to the bone. He was trouble with a capital T.

I blinked, snatching my hand back. "Don't count on it."

I stepped around him, and I could feel his eyes everywhere on my body as I eased my way through the crowd. My hands were trembling as if I were a junkie who needed a fix and mystery man was my heroin. By the time I made it out of the club, I was kicking myself for getting sucked in by his games.

What a total waste of damn time.

Pulling out my cell, I dialed Tabitha. "Hey, Tabi! Where the hell are you?"

"At the bar, looking for you. Where did you go? I came back, and you and the lion were both gone. Please tell me you decided to take him home."

Frantically, I waved down a cab. "Oh, hell no. He was too... everything. Look, I've got a raging headache. Give Mr. Steele my apology." I hopped into the cab and gave the driver my address.

Tabitha exhaled loudly. "No need. He couldn't make it. Just go home, and we'll reschedule."

"Later."

I shoved my cell into my bag and watched the blur of lights as the cab whizzed through the city. Finally approaching the treelined street where my townhouse—purchased when prices were low but poised to climb in the revitalized area in Manhattan—was located only a few steps from Central Park, I barely waited for the driver to stop before shoving the money at him and jumping out. Running up the stairs, I skidded to a stop, breaking out into a cold sweat at the sight of a vase of long-stemmed white roses sitting in front of my door.

"Oh God. Shit just got real." I pulled out the card, reading it aloud. "J."

Oh, hell no!

I grabbed the vase, stomped down the stairs, and dumped it into a trash can. I gritted my teeth, trying not to freak out as I went back upstairs and entered my house.

How the hell did Jaxon find me?

My body shivered with disgust, remembering how the utter madness had spiraled out of control after he'd broken in to Jade's apartment and left the rose and my underwear on my bed.

I'd lived through agonizing months of huge, elaborate vases filled with white roses being delivered to me every day with one creepy sentence scribbled on each card—*Love you. J.*

Even now, the mere scent of roses made me queasy to the point of throwing up.

When the roses had mysteriously stopped showing up, I'd thought the madness was over, but of course, I had been wrong. It had just begun. He'd shown up at every party I attended, and he'd chased away any guy who attempted to talk to me. When I confronted him—telling him to leave me alone—that only seemed to enrage him.

Paranoid that he'd been lurking in the shadows, waiting to hurt me, I'd locked myself away in my apartment, only venturing out for work. After weeks and months had passed without incident, I'd breathed a sigh of relief. I'd thought my world was safe again—until it had come crashing down.

I tried to fight the all-too-familiar dread that seeped into my bones. The memories lingered. The fear remained. Nothing could erase that day from my mind.

The day Jaxon had grabbed me, pulling me into a dark alleyway with a knife pressed against my throat. He'd babbled words of love over and over as he'd brutally ripped off my clothes with sick lust in his eyes. In that moment of total hopelessness, I'd known from his crazed stare that he actually thought he owned me. Bitterness had coated my tongue when I realized I was nothing but a piece of property to him, his possession that he had every intention of claiming repeatedly until I broke.

Tears had streamed down my face as I braced for the impending savage violation. Shivering on the cold ground, I'd turned my head away, letting my mind go blank. I'd known I would never be the same after this day. But when a lone homeless man had stumbled upon us, saving me, I'd been thrown a lifeline. Though, I knew Jaxon wasn't finished with me, and that had just been a momentary reprieve. Utter rage had clouded Jaxon's eyes before he'd sliced me across my shoulder.

His gaze had gone flat and hard. "Never forget, you'll always belong to me," he'd hissed before calmly walking away.

My thoughts snapped back to the present while I rubbed the light scar. "Never forget," I whispered, fighting the cold fear running down my spine.

Jaxon was back to claim what he thought was his—me. I was ready to fight as if my life depended on it. Because it did.

❧ *5* ❧

SINTHIA

I GULPED MY COFFEE, feeling like shit after tossing and turning all night. My thoughts were torn—half fretting over the horror of Jaxon's return, and the other half lingering over the sensual memory of the mystery man from last night. The only thing chasing away the craziness was reading the newspaper article before me.

First page! They put me on the first page.

I still couldn't believe the woman smiling up from the page, displaying pieces from her upcoming clothing line, was me. I was reeling from being interviewed by the most iconic newspaper in New York City when my thoughts were interrupted by my ringing cell.

"What's up, Cisco?"

"Hello, Sin, baby! Congrats on your interview. The phone hasn't stopped ringing all morning. We have lots of new clients booked for today," he stated matter-of-factly.

I loved Cisco, I really did, but he was a pushy pain in the ass. Our friendship worked well, but the business relationship was sorely lacking.

"Cisco, how many times have I asked you not to book clients without checking with me first?"

I could picture the adorable pout on his face when he said, "What would you have me do? They've been clamoring for a private session with you, and I booked them."

I sighed heavily, wavering between the daunting tasks of creating one-of-a-kind pieces for my private clients and finishing my collection.

I was grateful Cisco had given me the opportunity to sell my clothing in his boutique. It allowed me to cultivate my cult following of rich women who had everything—including catwalk queens and Jade, my in-house muse, all of whom thought nothing of splurging on my edgy clothing. My clients kept me well paid and living comfortably, but my unfinished collection was one step closer to my dream. And my dream was so close I could taste it.

"And it has nothing to do with the fact that you get a hefty commission from every new client, huh?" I knew I sounded grumpy, but I couldn't keep up with the rampant pace of new clients and complete my collection at the same time. Something had to give. "Cancel all the appointments, and don't book any clients until I tell you."

"Come on, Sin," he whined. "I need more pieces. I can't keep your clothing on my racks." He huffed. "Besides, you have to come in. Cate wants to discuss some design changes to her wedding gown."

I rolled my eyes. "Again?"

Agreeing to create a wedding gown for Cate, Jade's aunt, had been a big damn mistake, but I'd decided to do it because of my friendship with Jade.

"Cisco, I can't do it. I have to get my collection done."

"You know her. What Cate wants, Cate gets," Cisco responded dryly.

Sadly, it was the truth. Cate Bellisario was the most powerful member of the Bellisario family. She was beautiful, rich, conniving, and bored. She was currently using her status among the New York elite to get her fiancé—Bigsby Calhoune, a wealthy shipping mogul—elected as the next New York City mayor.

When Cate had revealed she wanted to walk down the aisle in a Sin Michaels creation, it hadn't exactly been a jumping-up-and-down moment for me. Every week, like clockwork, Cate would show up, unannounced, at my house to discuss her gown. Over time, those visits had turned into her giving me unsolicited business advice, even recommending I talk to Bigsby about investing in my "little fashion" business. I politely declined. Her slick-looking fiancé made me very uncomfortable, to say the least.

"Cisco, just cancel the appointment." My doorbell rang. "Look, I've got to go. I'll call you later."

I padded over to the door, knowing exactly who it was. Flinging the door open, I saw Jade bouncing up and down as she excitedly waved the newspaper like a flag.

"My Sin is in the newspaper," she squealed, pulling me in for a tight hug.

I stepped back with a wobbly smile as we dashed away the tears of joy. "Oh, don't get all emotional on me, actress extraordinaire."

Jade pouted playfully. "I can't help it. My best friend is on the front page of a major New York City newspaper."

"Yes, it's a change from seeing your gorgeous face staring up from the entertainment section."

It had been quite a year for Jade. She was on fire and was now starring in a smoking-hot television series. Not to mention, she'd been cast in three lead movie roles this year. I was so proud of her.

I pulled her in before closing the door behind her. "What are you doing here anyway? I thought you'd still be shooting that difficult scene you had so much angst about last night."

She smiled. "Nope. I dazzled them as usual, and we wrapped up early."

I walked over to the kitchen counter, picked up my cup, and

took a sip of coffee. "Never the modest one," I responded, smirking.

Jade playfully batted her eyes. "What? I'm the star of that damn show, and I'll never let them forget it."

"Uh-huh." I took another sip of coffee. "Help yourself to some."

She shook her head. "No coffee. You and I are going out to celebrate tonight. First, we'll have dinner, and then we'll hit the hookah bar."

I gestured to the mess of fabric scattered around my house that also doubled as my workspace. "I can't. I have to work."

Jade scrunched her nose. "Too much work—that's all you do now. I'm worried about you. You need to rest."

I waggled my eyebrows. "There's no rest for the wicked."

Jade frowned. "I'm not joking, Sin. You're headed for a major burnout."

I lifted my hands in surrender. "Okay. As soon as I launch my collection, I'll take a break. I promise."

"Bullshit. You're obsessed with impressing that pretentious bitch, Tabitha, and she's fixated on outshining you, her protégée." Jade jammed her hands on her hips. "I don't like or trust her."

I rolled my eyes. "You've made that abundantly clear from day one." Leaning over the counter, I pressed my forehead against the cool granite, feeling the migraine approaching.

Listening to Jade's and Tabitha's snide comments about each other was exhausting, and it was even more strenuous trying to keep them apart. Jade hated Tabitha's biting, acidic personality, and Tabitha resented Jade's privileged lifestyle. I was stuck in the middle of a pointless fight.

Why can't they just get along?

Jade drummed her manicured nails on the countertop. "And you're a stubborn ass who refuses to listen. I've seen the way she looks at you. It's creepy, like *The Silence of the Lambs* creepy. It's like she wants to rip off your skin and wear it like a fucking fur coat."

I snapped my head up, refusing to laugh at her joke. "I'm not even talking about this right now, Jade."

"Okay, well, let's talk about the mystery investor she hooked you up with. How did the meeting go last night?"

I hesitated. *Damn! She's got me on this one.* "You won the bet. He didn't show up. He had an emergency meeting."

She looked at me smugly. "Uh-huh. First, let's deal with what I get for winning our bet." She swayed toward the racks of clothing and pulled out the leather dress I'd worn last night. "I'll take this in cream and make it tight. I have a movie premiere next week, and I need to look smoking hot." She winked at me. "Oh, and you're coming as my guest. Feel free to sex it up with your outfit."

I rolled my eyes. "Anything else, Queen Jade?"

"Yes." Her eyes narrowed. "I call bullshit on that meeting last night. Either Tabitha is a fucking liar, or that investor is a shady fucker. I say yes to both."

My fists tightened. I knew exactly where she was going with this, and I didn't like it. "What do you want me to say, Jade? Money and family don't mix, so I couldn't take money from you."

Jade crossed her arms. "Couldn't or wouldn't?"

"Wouldn't. I know it would have been a loan, but it just didn't feel right." I paused, struggling with the words. "You've been right by my side through the shitstorm of my life. I love you for that and for...well, being you. I don't know where I'd be if I didn't have you in my life, kicking me in the ass when I wanted to give the hell up. But sink or swim, I needed to make this deal happen on my own." I bit my bottom lip. "Do you understand where I'm coming from?"

Jade sighed heavily before walking over to me and grabbing my hands. "I understand more than you think. You're a strong woman, Sin. If I weren't around, you would have survived." Tears spilled down her cheeks. "I can't say the same thing for myself.

You're my anchor. I wouldn't even be here if you hadn't walked into that restroom that day."

I sniffled. "Shit, now you're going to make me cry ugly tears."

Before that fateful day, I hadn't been a big believer in luck or that stupid fucking saying, "Everything happens for a reason." Then I'd walked into our high school restroom, and I'd seen a girl, Jade, lying on the floor with a needle stuck in her forearm. The EMT had said I saved her life. From that day forward, we'd become unlikely friends, tethered together by tragedy and fate. We pushed each other further. Our friendship tightened, creating a perfect synergy unmatched by any other relationship to date. We were an unstoppable team who stuck by each other no matter how rough the circumstances.

"It's no secret that I had a drug problem," Jade said. "You dragged me from the pits of hell when the lure of drugs had nearly drowned me. I almost died, but you saved me. You're not my best friend, Sin. You're my sister, and what is mine is yours. That's keeping it as real as it gets."

I tugged her hair playfully. "Why can't I stay mad at you?"

She gave me a hundred-watt smile. "Because I'm charismatic and beautiful." She hugged me quickly before pouring herself some coffee. "Tell me what else happened last night at the McKay Club. Did you see anything wickedly dirty that I can add to my sex position to-do list?"

I snorted. "Like you need help with that."

She winked. "I'm a student always willing to learn."

"Nope. I wasn't invited into the grown-up section." Absently, I rubbed the scar on my shoulder. "But something strange did happen when I got home. I think Jaxon's back."

Jade's eyes widened. "I, uh... Shit. This is bad." She fumbled with her mug as she plopped down onto a stool. "Why do you think he's back?"

"I came home to find a vase of white roses and a note with the letter *J* scribbled on it in front of my door."

Jade leaned forward. "I can't believe that bastard is back to stalking you. You need to go to the police."

"He's careful and diabolical. Even if I went to the police, what in the hell would I say?" I arched a brow. "Leaving a vase of roses on my doorstep is hardly grounds for filing a complaint." I sighed. "No, I'm going to have to wait for him to slip up."

"You need to stay with me." Jade's jaw tightened.

"I can protect myself, Jade. Shit, I've been doing a damn good job for twenty-six years."

Jade grabbed my arm. "Don't get all huffy. I'm worried."

I squeezed her arm gently. "I know. I'll be okay, I promise."

I stared off into space, fighting the urge to never leave the safety of my house again, but I'd come too far to ever let that shit happen. Now everything was finally going my way. It had been a hard road to success, but finally, the pain of my past was behind me. I was no longer the broken girl. I was strong and in control, and I refused to let Jaxon win.

❧ *6* ❧

SINTHIA

AFTER FINALLY KICKING Jade out so I could start my workday, I finished checking my emails, following up with possible buyers and distributors. Normally, during the initial stages of my collection, the majority of my day would be consumed with design work, closing myself off for at least two weeks just to focus on drawing and sorting through everything. But this time, the design work had already come together, and I was starting on a gown Jade would wear for her upcoming gala. The premiere of my gown would have the fashion hags salivating for the release of my collection, and I couldn't wait.

Sitting on the arm of my couch, I stared at the beginnings of the Sin Michaels collection, which were hanging on racks in parts of my four-thousand-square-foot townhouse. I exhaled a frustrated breath. I was going to have a busy day of working on toiles and cutting patterns.

My phone vibrated with a text from Cate.

We need to meet. I have design changes. Call me!

I stared at it with my fingers poised to text her back with two words—*Fuck off.*

I looked over at my sketchbook lying on the coffee table, and I stared at the wedding dress I'd designed for her.

She can kiss my ass.

I wasn't going to change another damn thing.

My temper was on the verge of flaring. I had so much work to do and so little time to let her take me out of my element.

I considered calling Giselle, my talkative intern who helped me most of the time, but then I changed my mind. I was already in a pretty fucked-up mood, and I needed to work in solitude. Turning on some music, I danced over to my workstation, ready to rock through the day, when my cell rang. I stared at the number I didn't recognize. Must be a new client, referred to me by Cisco.

"Sin Michaels," I chirped into the phone.

"Hello, Ms. Michaels. This is Ram Steele. I'm sorry we couldn't meet last night." His voice was smooth and easy.

I fumbled the phone. "Hold on." I ran over to my tablet and turned off the music. "Hello, Mr. Steele. I'm happy you called." I walked back over to my workstation while wiping my now sweaty palm against my jeans. "I wanted to talk to you. I'm not sure what your concerns are, but I assure you Sin Michaels Corporation is doing just fine—well, more than fine." I cleared my throat. "Did you see today's newspaper? I had a whole article giving kudos to my upcoming line."

"Yes, we did," he stated coolly. "But we have some major concerns that will delay us in giving you the additional money you requested."

Fuck. My. Life.

My heart clenched. Without that money, I would be screwed. I'd ordered expensive custom prints from a factory in Asia. One delayed payment could mean the fabric wouldn't arrive in time, halting my whole collection.

My stomach churned.

"What concerns?" I croaked.

"Business concerns that should be discussed in person," he stated calmly.

My fingers tightened around the workstation's edge. "Mr.

Steele, can I be blunt?" I tried to calm down, but the more I thought about the impact of his devastating announcement, the more pissed I grew.

"Please do."

"This is bullshit." I paced back and forth. "You gave me two million dollars, and per our agreement, you committed to giving me another million within six months."

"Ms. Michaels, did you actually read the agreement?" He paused. "Because if you did, you would know it contains a clause that entitles us not only to request our two million dollars back, with interest, but also to break the contract altogether."

I nearly swallowed my tongue.

Oh, hell no!

"Are you fucking kidding me? What in the world would make you want to do some dumb shit like that? We had a deal." There was no way that I was going to give up without fighting for my dream. I needed this damn money.

"I do respect your candor, Ms. Michaels." His voice was low and even, almost kind. "But that doesn't change the fact that we need to discuss our concerns in person. We'll meet today at three. Please take down this address."

I scribbled his directions with shaky fingers. "I'll be there at three sharp."

I disconnected and promptly dialed Tabitha.

"You've reached Tabitha Thorp. I'm away on a creative sabbatical. Please leave a message, and I'll get back to you when I return."

I stared at the phone. *Creative sabbatical? What. The. Fuck?*

I'd known her for years, and not once had she taken any sabbaticals.

Damn it!

I didn't know what was going on, but I felt like I was being royally screwed. I released a frustrated growl, and with a sweep of my arm, I knocked everything off my workspace.

❦   7   ❦

CORE

I SNAPPED my head up when my office door opened, and Ram, my business partner, walked in before closing the door behind him with a decisive click.

"That was the most fucked-up thing you've ever asked me to do," Ram snarled.

I arched a brow. "The hell it was." Pushing aside the contract on my desk, I waited for the brewing tirade I knew was on the tip of Ram's tongue.

"Okay, not the most fucked-up thing, but a damn close second." Ram sat down, running a hand over his head. "I still don't get it." He paused. "What the hell is this Sinthia Michaels shit about?"

I remained silent for a few minutes, trying not to lose my patience. No one in the McKay organization would dare question me this way except Ram. Our years of connection as friends and business partners had given him that right.

Ram kicked his feet up onto my desk. "Don't give me that fucking stare, bro. I want to know. What the hell possessed you to give a fashion designer two million dollars?"

I leaned back in my chair. "You should know me by now. I don't give shit away. I invested two million dollars," I snapped.

Ram scoffed. "Well, you invested a shitload of money into a clothing business, and I'm pretty sure that was a dumbass decision. That pussy must be serious."

I shrugged. "Fuck the two million. I spend that much on the upkeep of my house in the south of France. The money is nothing compared to what I stand to gain if my hunch turns out to be right."

I still marveled at the fact that I'd come a long way, going from a vicious criminal thug to a legitimate businessman. Now powerful and rich, I could invest millions in a business that I thought would make a profit for me.

"This is bullshit, Core. You invested in a business you don't give a shit about. Why?"

My temper flared. "You're pushing the boundaries of our friendship, Ram."

Ram leaned forward. "Like I give a shit. We're family, and family asks questions."

I closed my eyes in irritation before snapping them open. "I finally found him—Bigsby Calhoune, the man we've been searching years for. He's been right under our noses."

Ram sucked in a quick breath. "Bigsby Calhoune? The man running for mayor? How did you come to that damn conclusion?" He blinked rapidly, followed by an open stare.

"Remember the charity event you couldn't attend?" I asked with a sharp tone.

8

CORE

Manhattan. Nights Ago.

Flanked by my enforcers—who roughed up my enemies and kept my business associates in line—brothers, Max and Rocco, I exited my luxury vehicle.

"Wait here," I instructed them. "I'll be in and out of this place in fifteen minutes."

I didn't normally mingle with New York's elite, and I damn sure never did political fundraising events. I'd only accepted tonight's invitation as a courtesy to Mitch Fillion. Mitch had stepped in and provided assistance with the legalities of a complicated and contentious company takeover that had been on the verge of crumbling. Mitch had proven to be more valuable and ruthless than I'd expected. I needed to keep men like Mitch—those who only cared about money, power, and status— in my pocket.

I watched the crazy scene progress. Overflowing into the street, New York's elite were sauntering into the invite-only, fifty-grand-per-plate dinner that was being hosted by Mitch in honor of his newest pet project—mayoral hopeful Bigsby Calhoune.

Adjusting my bow tie, I strode confidently by the frenzied mess of paparazzi, who ignored me in favor of the star-studded elite, preening before the flashing cameras. I hated the press. Unlike most men with my wealth and power who gravitated toward the ego-stroking media, I avoided them like the plague, living my life in anonymity.

I waited impatiently while a white-gloved security staffer politely scanned my body with a handheld metal detector. Entering through the huge front doors, I immediately moved through the room—a cavernous, modern space with large columns and slab granite. The private, formal political party was in full swing as men in tuxedos escorted their diamond-encrusted ladies around the room like arm candy.

Blending smoothly into a throng of foreign dignitaries, businessmen, and socialites, I headed for the bar, ordered a drink, and absorbed the high-octane mixture of new oil money and old European wealth before the bartender pushed a glass of scotch between my fingers. The cigar-smoking men talked business as their beautiful flavors of the month looked on with blank faces, casually taking a glass of champagne or a canapé from the passing waiters.

Glittering, sleek women with strikingly sculpted faces smiled provocatively at me while circling around me in hopes of snagging husband number two or three. My eyes roamed over them with disinterest. They looked like most women I'd fucked over the years during my transition from crime lord to legitimate business mogul. Along with surgically enhanced breasts provided by top plastic surgeons, they all had hard bodies courtesy of hours in the gym with their personal trainers.

I was bored with the selection.

Sipping my scotch, I ignored them. Until now, it hadn't occurred to me that I hadn't fucked anyone who looked remotely like a real woman in a while. Even with a string of women and business successes over the years, I found I actually missed one thing from my days as the ruthless leader of the largest crime empire in New York—a woman with soft curves, pretty, girl-next-door looks, and a sassy, take-no-shit personality. Maybe it was time for a change, but finding a woman who could satisfy my distinct and dark sexual tastes would be nearly impossible.

My thoughts were interrupted by Mitch's loud, animated introduction of the well-matched, beautiful couple—Cate Bellisario and Bigsby Calhoune—to a guest. Bored, I watched Bigsby shake the guest's hand with an exaggerated flourish.

My body tensed.

My mind flared with recognition at the unmistakable glint of diamonds and rubies on Bigsby's middle finger.

Pushing away from the bar with adrenaline coursing through my veins, I walked leisurely through the crowd and toward the trio. The guests shifted, cutting off my view of Mitch and the couple, but I easily found them again and confidently strode up to them.

"Core." Mitch was all smiles as he shook my hand. "I'm glad you could make it tonight."

Bigsby's eyes narrowed on my all-seeing-eye neck tattoo. As Bigsby frowned, his gaze darted to Mitch. He clearly did not approve of my presence at his dinner event.

My expression darkened. "Is there a problem?"

Mitch shot Bigsby an irritated glare before laughing loudly. He clapped me on the back. "Apologies, Core." He gave Bigsby an admonishing stare. "Bigsby is new to the intricacies and important players of our circle, so please excuse his ignorance. I'm still trying to get him up to speed."

Bigsby's body tightened as he ran his hand over his salt-and-pepper hair with agitation.

Mitch looked pointedly at the couple. "This is Core McKay—as in McKay Corporation. He's one of my biggest clients."

Cate's mask of neutrality slipped as her eyes widened. "Well, this night is full of surprises. I get the privilege of putting a face to the renowned name." She smiled. "Congrats on your recent billion-dollar merger."

I inclined my head but remained silent.

Mitch looked at me eagerly. "This is Cate Bellisario."

Cate nodded politely as I swept my gaze over her. From her formfitting designer dress to her perfectly coiffed hair and artfully applied makeup, she was the very image of New York socialite success. I smirked. I knew her perfection was a facade for the seedy dark side she kept hidden from her fiancé. On several occasions, the smoldering nymph had trolled my sex club, begging Ram to top her. The duality of her flawless persona amused me.

Bigsby cleared his throat. "I'm Bigsby Calhoune." He smiled as he offered his hand to me before shaking it enthusiastically. "I apologize. I thought I knew most of Mitch's friends."

My face was a cold mask, barely hiding my disdain. "Leave the thinking to Mitch and your fiancée. You're way out of your depth, Mr. Calhoune." I stepped back, sipping my scotch.

Bigsby shifted uncomfortably before looking to Mitch for assistance, but none came. I knew Mitch expected Bigsby to grovel and make amends for his slight against me.

Bigsby's smile was forced as he said, "Cate says I'm like a bull in a china shop at these events. Apologies, Mr. McKay."

I tilted my head. "You're from Brooklyn," I stated matter-of-factly.

Bigsby looked visibly startled. "Uh…yes. How did you know?"

I stared at him shrewdly. "You're trying too hard to hide the accent." Effectively dismissing him, I turned to Mitch. "You pulled out the big guns tonight. You must think he's a winner."

Mitch beamed at Bigsby. "You're damn right. If I have anything to do with it, Bigsby will be New York's next mayor."

"I wouldn't start writing acceptance speeches. I know his opponent personally. He's thorough and ruthless." I narrowed my eyes on Bigsby. "And his specialty is unearthing his opponent's skeletons."

Bigsby's grin slipped before his lips curled up into a stiff smile.

I winked at Cate while addressing Bigsby. "I hope your beautiful fiancée has taken care to bury them deep."

Bigsby wrapped a possessive hand around her narrow waist.

I glanced at the chunky gold ruby-and-diamond-encrusted horseshoe ring on Bigsby's middle finger. "That's a unique ring you have there, Calhoune. It's one of a kind, I'm sure."

Bigsby smiled cockily. "Yes, it is. I've had it for over forty years. It's custom-made." He looked over at Cate. "And I'll never take it off."

Cate sighed heavily, looking at the gaudy ring with disgust. "Believe me, I've tried."

Bigsby winked at Cate. "It's my good luck charm. You will have to pry it off my dead body, sweetheart."

She stared back with a simple look and said plainly, "Do I really have to wait that long?"

Bigsby laughed loudly. "You're such a minx."

Mitch waved to someone across the room and then looked over at me apologetically. "Can you excuse us? We need to make the rounds before dinner is served."

"I'm leaving anyway. I have important business to attend to," I responded.

Mitch looked disappointed. "I seated you at our table with Cate and Bigsby, but I understand." He started to usher the couple away. "We'll talk this week."

Exiting the venue, trying hard to contain my building rage, I pulled out my cell and barked, "Kevin, dig up everything you can on Bigsby Calhoune."

MY MIND SNAPPED BACK TO THE PRESENT. UNCLASPING MY

fingers, I said to Ram, "The plan is now in motion. After all these years, we've finally found the ring. What are the odds of that?"

Ram leaned forward. "We've been searching for that shit for years, and it's been right under our noses." He paused. "So what's Sinthia's connection?"

"I don't know. Kevin dug up some interesting intel about Bigsby looking into Sinthia Michaels's business. If he's interested in her and her business, there has to be a pretty damn good reason." I leaned back in my chair, smiling coldly. "Now he has to deal directly with me."

When I'd gotten the call from Kevin about Bigsby's interest in Sinthia, my first question had been, *Who the fuck is Sinthia Michaels?*

It hadn't taken Kevin long to do a thorough investigation, but he hadn't found anything linking Bigsby to her. I had known, though, that if Bigsby was interested in Sinthia, there had to be a sinister motive, which was why I had to acquire Sinthia Michaels's business fast. I'd had Kevin search through her background again, looking for anything that could be used as leverage. Surprisingly, Sinthia was squeaky-clean and free from scandal. Frustrated and running out of time and options, I found a chink in her armor—money.

She needed money, and I had lots of it. But to my frustration, I couldn't find a way to get into Sinthia's small inner circle without raising suspicion or scaring her off.

That was when Kevin had found the game changer—Tabitha Thorp. I had known Tabitha from the old neighborhood. When we were young, we had hung out in the same criminal circles. The only difference was, back then, the now-famous Tabitha had worked as a drug mule for her seedy drug kingpin boyfriend, Ben Vargos. I knew Tabitha. I'd even fucked her several times behind Ben's back. She was a money-hungry whore who could be easily manipulated.

So when I found out the currently successful Tabitha Thorp

owed a shitload of money to her unsavory criminal ex-boyfriend, Ben, I swooped in.

One call later, I'd recruited Tabitha to help me get close to Sinthia. Tabitha had convinced Sinthia of the value of getting an investor—specifically, me—to help her expand her business. In exchange, I'd agreed to pay off Tabitha's debt to Ben and send her on a very long vacation.

Bigsby was a dirty criminal underneath his slick, cleaned-up politician veneer. I still couldn't figure out why Bigsby's socialite fiancée, Cate, would marry a lowlife, but she had cleaned Bigsby up like some stray puppy she'd found on the street. She'd gotten Bigsby a well-paid publicist, and she was now helping him run for mayor.

"Bigsby Calhoune might have a new identity and life, but he's still the power-hungry thug who killed my mother and left me to die. He's going to pay for what he did," I hissed.

I had thought of nothing but revenge for years. It consumed me. Just thinking about the night when the unknown assailant had shot both Mom and me fueled my hate fire. Mom had died, but I survived.

I stood up, absently tracing the scar across my brow while staring at the Manhattan skyline. "Bigsby is unfinished business. Business I've been waiting to resolve for far too many years."

"I saw the picture and read the newspaper article about Sinthia Michaels. But what does she really look like?" Ram asked.

I shrugged. "A stunner with curves in all the right fucking places."

"A stunner?" Ram laughed. "I've heard you describe women as fuckable, but never a stunner." He paused. "Interesting."

"There's nothing interesting about it. She's definitely fuckable, but I don't mix business with pleasure, especially not this business."

"I see."

I looked over my shoulder. "It's not that deep, Ram."

Ram snorted. "A fuckable stunner? Well, that's a game changer when it comes to your track record with women."

"I'm going nowhere near Sinthia Michaels. I don't need the complication." Turning back around, I continued to stare at the skyline.

My life was difficult enough, and I didn't need any distractions, particularly now that I'd found Mom's killer. Besides, I wasn't relationship material. I never was and never would be.

Watching Mom getting killed had changed me, shaping me into the man I was today—a sadistic, driven, ruthless, cold, and heartless killer. I was the product of my environment. Growing up in a run-down part of Manhattan and fighting every kid on the block who would talk shit about my young, single mother, who had performed at strip clubs to earn a living, had done that to me.

At a young age, I'd seen and lived through shit most people would only see in movies. Those things were not easily forgotten —like people being gunned down ruthlessly in broad daylight or single mothers giving blow jobs in alleyways so they could pay rent and put food on the table.

I had come a long way from those days and now had more money than I could ever spend, but the fucked-up memories remained. I would never forget where I'd come from or the day when my world had changed forever, leading me to the ultimate task before me—avenging my mother's murder.

Even after all these years, the details of that fateful day were burned into my memory... I had been doing my homework when I heard Mom's blood-curdling scream. I remembered running from the living room into the kitchen where I saw her being pinned against the wall by a big, burly man whose back was facing me while he repeatedly beat Mom's face to a pulp. I charged, jumping onto the man's back while trying to claw his eyes out of his head.

I could still hear the bone-crunching thud Mom's frail body made as the man slammed her to the floor.

The man swung around and yelled at me, "You little bastard, you're dead!" He grabbed me by the neck before throwing me clear across the kitchen.

My head had smashed against the corner of the kitchen counter before my body bounced onto the floor.

Dazed, I slowly reached my hand up to my head. I felt the oozing thickness of gushing blood across my eyebrow, but I refused to give in to the pain. Mom needed me.

My heart had leaped out of my chest when my mother screamed, "Leave my son alone, you fucking bastard. This is between you and me, damn coward."

The man charged at her, pulling a .357 Magnum from his belt-line. "Shut the fuck up, whore. You brought this on yourself. I warned you to keep your damn mouth shut!" he yelled while grabbing her by the hair with one hand.

Turning her face away from him, the man had placed the gun to her head. It had seemed like an eternity to me as I stared at the gold ruby-and-diamond-encrusted horseshoe ring on the man's middle finger before he fired the gun, killing Mom. He then stormed over to me with his gun aimed toward me before squeezing off some rounds, and then my world had gone completely dark.

I had been near death when Ram found me choking on my blood on the gore-soaked kitchen floor, but it had been too late for Mom. Ram saved my life, and we made a pact that day. The man who killed my mother would pay with his life.

Young, wild, and ruthless, Ram and I had risen quickly in the world of organized crime, building our empire from the bottom. As the years passed, we never forgot the man without a face, only knowing him by his ruby-and-diamond ring.

Our criminal territory had expanded. Life and money had been good, but we knew we had to get out or we'd end up like so many of our friends—dead or in jail. So it hadn't been a hard choice to decriminalize our business and turn our lives around, but I wouldn't rest until I made the man with the ring pay.

"Sinthia Michaels is all business, and I'm willing to destroy her business in order to take down Bigsby," I retorted.

Ram's face tightened. "You know how I feel about this shit. We've been through hell and back together, so there's no question about me helping you take him down. But this is between you, me, and him. No one else. Cut the Sinthia Michaels chick loose."

My temper flared. "I don't give a shit about her," I snarled.

I needed Sinthia Michaels as bait, and if that meant she might become a casualty in my war against Bigsby, then so be it.

"She's already involved whether she knows it or not, and I have no intention of letting her go until I get what I want—Bigsby." I pulled out a cigar. "Now we've got lots of work to do. We need to call every retailer that we own a major stake in and let them know the Sinthia Michaels deal doesn't happen until we personally approve it."

❧ 9 ❧

SINTHIA

LESS THAN THREE HOURS LATER, the cab pulled up in front of the huge building. My stomach was queasy. My head throbbed as I gawked at the structure.

I looked into the rearview mirror, meeting the gaze of the cab driver. "Are you sure this is the right place?"

The driver drummed his fingers against the steering wheel. "Lady, this is the address you gave me." He jabbed a big finger toward the sign. "See that? McKay Corporation."

I frowned. "This can't be right."

"Young lady, if you want to go to another address, tell me where to go. If not, pay the fare."

I bit my lower lip. "No, I'm good." I paid before hopping out.

Pulling damp tendrils of hair away from my neck, I stared at the huge sign, *McKay Corporation*, as if it were a mirage. A shiver of trepidation ran down my spine.

This was all wrong—first the Ram call, then Tabitha's disappearing act, and now this. Someone was fucking with me, and I wanted to know who and why. Pulling myself to my full height, I walked confidently through the glass doors and over to the guest desk.

"I'm here to see Mr. Steele." I tapped my fingers on the counter, hoping the man would say I was in the wrong building.

The guard looked at me blankly. "Ms. Michaels, ID, please."

Shit. I'm at the right building.

Fumbling inside my handbag, I pulled out my driver's license and handed it over. "Here."

He glanced at it briefly. Then he scanned my license through a device on his tablet before smoothly tapping the on-screen keyboard.

I frowned. "What are you doing with my information?"

"Just a security precaution, Ms. Michaels. We record the information of everyone who enters this building." He nodded toward the elevator as he returned my license. "Top floor."

The elevator ride up to Steele's office was the longest one I'd ever taken. I wasn't sure what was going on, but I didn't like it one bit. If Mr. Steele thought he could just screw me on this deal without a fight, he was damn mistaken. I was prepared to do battle.

The elevator dinged, and I stepped out into the palatial suite decorated with ornate, eighteenth-century furniture. My eyes immediately went to the office door guarded by two well-dressed, armed men.

"Is this an office or a high-security prison?" I mumbled under my breath.

I walked down a long hallway, passing by a massive glass conference room. My sway became deliberately more sensual when I noticed a striking woman sitting behind a large desk, scrutinizing me with frank disapproval. She scanned my outfit of skintight leather leggings paired with a black T-shirt and tailored jacket. I didn't give a shit. I had plenty of appropriate business attire, but I'd promised myself years ago that I wouldn't dress or act a certain way to please anyone but myself. I kept it real. If Mr. Steele didn't like it, he could kiss my ass.

I stopped before her desk. "I'm here to see Ram Steele."

"Have a seat, Ms. Michaels," she responded with a British accent.

Giving her a cold smile, I responded with, "Thanks, but I'll stand."

"Your prerogative," she huffed.

Just to get under her skin, I swayed over to the cushy chairs, making sure that my ridiculously high stilettos tapped loudly on the marble floor.

"Shh!" she snapped with an admonishing glare.

I snickered. *What an uptight wench.* I could just imagine what Mr. Steele was like. He was probably some uptight billionaire who was so old his bones cracked when he walked.

I turned my head in the direction of the huge office door that had just opened. My eyes widened at the sight of the tall, lean, and exceedingly handsome man striding toward me.

Jesus, he's hot enough to make panties melt.

He tilted his head curiously as he greeted me coldly. "Please come in, Ms. Michaels. Mr. McKay is waiting."

I recognized his voice—Ram Steele. I quirked a brow. "What's going on?"

Silently, he motioned me to enter the office.

"I asked you a question, Mr. Steele," I snapped.

Mr. Steele heaved a long-suffering sigh before pressing a gentle hand against the middle of my back, nudging me into the office. "Ms. Michaels, a word of advice—if I were you, I would play nice with him. He's in a real fucked-up mood today," he said, his voice clipped, before closing the door behind him with a decisive click.

Play nice?

Not a damn chance.

I was ready for a fight. Squaring my shoulders, I found my eyes drawn to a man in a tailored business suit, standing with his hands clasped behind his back as he looked out the window. His large, muscular frame would have intimidated anyone, but I refused to be cowed by him. Taking a deep, calming breath, I walked toward the middle of the room and stopped.

"Sinthia Michaels," he said in a low-pitched voice that sent delicious chills down my spine. "Have you brought my money?" he asked in a gravelly voice that sounded vaguely familiar.

My mouth opened and shut, not believing what he'd just asked. "Money? What money?"

He turned from the window and looked straight at me. I nearly swallowed my tongue. It was the man from last night.

"You're Core McKay?" I took a step forward, compelled by the invisible string drawing me to him.

His gaze was intimidating and unrelenting. "Good to see you again, Ms. Michaels." His booming deep voice resonated throughout the office. "Have a seat. We have a lot to discuss."

His eyes traveled all the way down my body. His predatory stare made me feel like a mouse beneath the bloodthirsty gaze of a cat. In the light of day, he was even more fucking menacing. His body was pure, rippling muscle—not workout-five-days-a-week-at-the-gym buff, but more like mixed martial arts, fucking-kick-motherfucker's-asses-just-for-the-fun-of-it buff. But it was his searing gray eyes that told the real story.

Core McKay was not a man to fuck with.

I hesitated, but I needed to get my bearings before I passed out from stress. "Fine," I conceded, taking a seat. "Listen, I'm going to cut to the fucking chase," I said. "Why the fuck am I here?"

He regarded me for a long time and then sat in the chair behind his mammoth desk. He smoothed the sleeves of his tailored shirt before running a hand across his blunt-cut, midnight-black hair. "Unfortunately, some disturbing information has recently come to my attention, and it makes me question your ability to make me a profit." His words were civil, but his eyes were hard as granite.

Oh, hell no! There is no way in hell I'm going to let him punk me like I'm some prison-yard bitch.

In a gesture of defiance, I raised my chin and met his gaze. "No offense, Mr. McKay, but my business deal is with MK Partners."

He actually smirked like he found me mildly amusing.

My eyes widened when it dawned on me. *Motherfucker!*

"Yes, Ms. Michaels, MK Partners is my investment company," he drawled.

I shook my head. *Oh shit. Please say it's not true.* My throat went completely dry as I felt like the walls were closing in around me. Still, I refused to roll over and surrender. I was a damn fighter.

"While that might be true, our agreement was not a loan. I would never take a loan from a man like you."

His eyes hardened.

Well, it was true. I had been hard up for an investor, but even I hadn't been that desperate—or stupid. I knew about the McKay Corporation and the rumors circulating about the mysterious and eccentric owner, Core McKay. He'd built his billion-dollar empire using drug trafficking, money laundering, and prostitution, and that was only to mention a few of the criminally speculated trades.

His jaw tightened. He was pissed, and it was damn scary.

"In your desperation to finance your business, you obviously lowered your fucking highbrow standards," he ground out. "Now the only thing I don't own is your company name. Other than that, I own ninety-seven percent of your precious enterprise."

My breath stuck in my throat. The silence stretched between us. My failure to look over the fine print of the contract was coming back to bite me in the ass. *Shit.*

"Impossible," I denied.

He gestured to the neatly stacked paperwork on his desk. "The impossible became possible, Ms. Michaels." His eyes flashed before he crossed his muscular arms, his biceps bulging.

He reminded me of a tiger patiently stalking its prey, and in his case, that was me.

I squared my shoulders before snatching the stack off the

desk. I scanned the paperwork slowly, stopping at the fine print. *Shit, it is a loan. How the fuck did I miss this?*

My gaze stopped on the name right next to my signature —*Core McKay.*

My stomach rolled. "This is a huge mistake. This wasn't supposed to be a loan. It was a deal for seven percent of my future earnings." I shook my head.

"Sinthia," he said my name as if testing it on his tongue. "Is that your signature?"

I tightened my lips, fighting back the impending flood of tears. "I swear, this was not what I thought I was agreeing to."

He inclined his head slightly. "Let this be a lesson. Read things thoroughly before you sign."

This just didn't make sense. *Why didn't Tabitha tell me my investor was McKay?*

I bit my lip, thinking about that day she'd brought me the contract. My stomach dropped when I remembered she'd seemed entirely too happy. In fact, come to think of it, she had been practically giddy that she'd found me the deal I needed to solve all my business problems.

He looked at me coldly. "Can you pay back my two million dollars plus interest today?"

Now he was toying with me.

He knew damn well I didn't have the money, and I sure as hell couldn't get it.

In desperation mode, I shifted my thoughts immediately to Jade, but I couldn't borrow the money from her because her assets were tied up in a big business venture to take the script she wrote and independently produce the film version.

I sputtered, "What the fuck do you want, McKay? Because —" I stopped mid-sentence, feeling warm and tingly as he stared at me with hooded eyes.

His physical magnetism was palpable. I swallowed hard, trying not to squirm under his sensuous stare.

Bastard. He wants me to beg. Well, that shit isn't happening.

Our eyes locked.

"I know you don't expect me to fuck you so you'll forget about this whole loan thing?"

He actually laughed at me as if I'd just told a joke. The sly sound ruffled my nerves.

"Do you really think I have to pay to get fucked?" he replied.

Such an arrogant ass.

I ground my teeth. "Then what do you want?"

"Not a damn thing but my money plus interest." He narrowed his eyes. "I'm not sure you're able to produce a profit, darling. My sources tell me your retailers are getting cold feet about the viability of your collection. They're pulling out of your deals."

I flinched like he'd physically slapped me. "Bullshit! I have concrete agreements with each of them."

"You really don't know shit about contracts. Nothing in business is concrete. That's what loopholes and a shitload of well-paid lawyers are for." He shot me an irritated glare. "I can tell you don't believe the shit I'm saying, so call Lily Sanchez."

I narrowed my eyes. "How do you know Lily?" I asked with disbelief ringing in my voice.

He shrugged. "Just call her." He cocked his head. "She'll confirm the gravity of your situation."

I pulled out my cell. My fingers trembled, but I willed them to stop. I would not break down in front of this prick. I called her.

"Hello, Sin. How are you?" Lily asked.

"Shitty. Look, is everything good to go with my collection deal?"

Lily cleared her throat. My stomach dropped.

"I was going to call you, Sin. I don't know what the hell is going on, but the financial planners are seriously discussing backing out of your deal."

I jumped up, turning my back on Core. "What the hell happened?" I whispered.

"Don't know. I'm still trying to find out. All I know is this is bigger than you or me."

My shoulders slumped. Her store was my biggest account.

"I'm two million in, Lily. My collection is almost complete. That's months of work. Do you understand me? Set up a meeting with the financial planners," I snapped.

"I'm sorry, Sin. My hands are tied. Give me a couple days to figure this out."

I stood there in shock after our call ended.

How in the world could my life have turned from rosy to shitty in a matter of hours?

I could feel Core's heated stare scorching through my clothes. I gathered my strength and turned around, feeling the noose tightening. It was time to make a deal with the devil. But before I did, I just had one question.

I lifted my chin. "How do you know Tabitha?"

He gave me a hard smile.

My eyes widened. "Oh, I see. You're one of her many fuck buddies." My voice was tight with accusation.

He straightened to his full, intimidating height. "Let's cut to the chase, shall we? I've known Tabitha for years in various... capacities. That's why she came to me when you had financing issues. She knew I was in the market for another lucrative invest-ment." He pulled out a cigar. "I did some extensive investigation of you and your company, and you are very talented." He lit his cigar. "But obviously, you're very naïve when it comes to business."

I tightened my fists.

I am going to fucking cunt-punch Tabitha when I find her.

"So you know where she is?" I hissed.

His lips twitched into a mockery of a smile. "Don't know, and I don't care. But when you find her, give her my regards." He paused, looking at me coolly. "Sinthia, you're tougher than I thought. I like that." He took a puff of the cigar. "I've come to a decision." He blew a ring of smoke before placing the cigar in the ashtray.

"What decision?" I barked. "You already made a decision when you gave me the two million dollars. Now you're making another decision?" I sneered.

"I will make it really simple for you." He crossed his arms and widened his stance. "I've invested two million into your business, and I intend on getting it back plus a hefty profit. I will retain full control of your company."

I nearly choked on my own breath. "This is bullshit! This is my business," I protested.

His eyes were ice-cold and distant when he continued, "Kevin, my accountant, will take care of all financial matters, including providing the money to continue your line. In addition, I will make some calls to my contacts to see if we can get your retailers back on board."

I licked my lips. His eyes fell to my mouth.

"And all of this is coming at what price?" My back stiffened and my eyes narrowed. "I will not use my company as a front for illegal business dealings."

His gray eyes narrowed. "What the fuck are you talking about?"

I closed my eyes tightly to block the sight of his hateful presence. "I worked too fucking hard to have my business and my name tied to anything illegal." I forced myself to look at him again.

He stalked over to me, his gaze blatantly ogling my body. "What a beautiful hypocrite. There was no thought about where the money was coming from when you took it. Now you're looking at me like I'm the fucking scum of the earth?"

He regarded me silently. It irritated me that he could unnerve me with just one look.

"I'm just calling it like I see it, Mr. McKay. I will not use my business for anything illegal."

He scowled. "Many years ago, I might have used you for that...and more. But now I'm a legitimate businessman."

My stomach twisted into knots. I was between a rock and a hard place, and legally, there was nothing I could do.

"What else do you want, McKay?" I asked.

I licked my bottom lip anxiously at the strange surges of energy rolling off him in waves.

His eyes roamed from my face to my body and then back again. "Oh, darling, I can't begin to tell you all the things I want from you. They would send your gorgeous ass running from this room. But the question is, what do you want, Ms. Michaels?"

Is he out of his damn mind?

As hot as he was, I wouldn't fuck him even if his cock were made of solid gold.

"I want you to let me out of this fucking deal," I grumbled.

McKay laughed coldly. "Not going to happen. Next," he all but sneered.

"If you wanted to, you could," I responded.

His expression revealed nothing. "I'm in the business of making money, not losing it. The deal remains." There was a tight note in his voice.

Lifting my chin, I continued to hold his stare. For several minutes, I didn't say anything as he continued to watch me.

"This is fucking ridiculous," I snapped. "It might be illegal too."

"Even you don't really believe that shit." The hardness of his voice sent chills down my spine.

I bit back the expletive hovering on my tongue. I knew I would be tied to him forever. Judging by his focused gaze, that was exactly what he wanted.

"And how long is this business arrangement going to last?"

"Until I determine the debt has been paid in full," he bit out letting his words sink in for a few seconds.

My blood froze in my veins. "Fuck you! You might own the company, but you don't own me."

His hands clenched and unclenched before he caught me by the arm and pressed me against the wall. In one swift move, he pinned my arms above my head. His tongue swept into my mouth while his other hand grabbed the back of my head with unleashed fury.

The last shreds of my ironclad control disintegrated as his mouth devoured and stroked me with a restrained sensuality that made my cunt clench from emptiness.

I opened my mouth wider, and I pushed my tongue into his. I groaned, tasting the hint of coffee and cigar. My head spun out of control as I kissed him back with all the pent-up anger, passion, and the most damning attraction that I had been denying.

Shamefully, I wanted him like no other.

My stomach plummeted with the sudden realization that this man would be my undoing.

As if he could read my mind, he broke off the kiss abruptly and stared at me with knowing, hard eyes. "I might not own you now, but I will," he responded with a steely voice before stepping back from me.

I stood there against the wall, trembling like a fool, as I watched him turn around and stride over to his wall of floor-to-ceiling windows.

"Now you may go, Ms. Michaels," he hissed, effectively dismissing me.

For several minutes, I just stared at his wide back in shock. Finally, I gathered what was left of my pride and walked out of the room.

On shaky legs, I stepped into the elevator and pressed my head against the wall as my mind clouded over with confusion.

I swallowed hard as the door slid closed.

Just when I thought I'd made peace with the universe and success was within my reach, fate had thrown me the ultimate middle finger.

Tears rolled down my cheeks as regret and dread washed over me.

I just made a deal with the fucking devil.

~

THANK YOU FOR READING **TWISTED LIES!**

More Core and Sin goodness continues with **TWISTED LIES 2!**

And sign up for my newsletter to find out about new books...

www.sedonavenez.com/newsletter

ABOUT THE AUTHOR

USA TODAY BESTSELLING AUTHOR SEDONA VENEZ lives in New York City with her hot ex-military hubby—hooah—and their fur babies. She loves writing sizzling, sexy intricate stories about strong but broken characters who push limits, overcome their fears and risk it all for love.

Sedona loves to connect with readers!
www.sedonavenez.com

OTHER TITLES BY SEDONA VENEZ

Aliens!

Paranormal Romance
Shifter Alphas Furever Series

Paranormal Romance
Credence Curse Series

Werewolves!
Wolf Elite Series

Operation Wolf: Gunner
Operation Wolf: Eli
Operation Wolf: Hunter
Wolf Elite - The Box Set

Bears!
Bear Elite Series
Operation Bear

Dark Romance
Dirty Secrets Series
Twisted Lies
Twisted Lies 2
Twisted Lies 3
Twisted Lies 4
Dirty Secrets - The Box Set

Contemporary Romance (MFM Ménage)
Standalone
Shameless Desires

Billionaire Romance
Standalone
Mr. Billionaire CEO

Urban Fantasy Romance
Magic Fire Collection

EXCERPT: TAMING THE BEAST

Want to sample a new series? Check out my Credence Curse books including this book, <u>Taming the Beast</u>.

I was stark naked—again. With huge ebony breasts swaying, ass jiggling, and designer stiletto-encased feet slapping against the dewy grass, I sauntered over to the center of the clearing.

Perching myself on top of the smooth boulder—or what I now lovingly called my rock of shame—I surveyed my recurring fixation.

My heart seemed to freeze and then pound. "Damn. You're such a beautiful kitty," I whispered.

Water cascaded off the tiger's magnificent reddish-rusty coat with narrow dark-brown stripes as he prowled out of the river toward me with rippling muscles. Its chest, throat, muzzle, and the insides of its limbs were creamy with a milky-colored area above the eyes that spread onto his cheeks.

When I extended my hand, he tilted his large head down, rubbing against it with a chuff-chuff sound.

"Hello, my big kitty. I'm happy to see you again, too," I answered his greeting. My digits trailed up to the white spot present on the back of its ear.

He nudged my hand away before circling me, his fur

caressing my bare legs while I admired the prominent ruff on his head and long tail ringed with noticeable dark bands.

Warmth radiated throughout my body as his fur deliciously tickled me.

"Every dream, you bring me here to watch you swim, and I still don't know why."

My mouth fell open when a deer pranced up to the river and drank from it, completely oblivious to the tiger's presence.

The tiger stilled, waited, and then pounced. The deer didn't even have a chance to run away before the tiger's big-as-saucers paws latched on to its hindquarters, bringing down the deer. The tiger gripped its neck, delivering a crushing bite to its prey. The deer stopped thrashing.

My fingers touched my parted lips before I closed them. "Holy shit."

This was a new addition to my nightly dreams. He'd never killed game before.

Wasting no time, the tiger dragged its dinner toward me, laying the carcass at my feet like an offering.

I gave him a weak half smile, trying desperately not to hurl at the sight of the dead deer. "Thank you, kitty, but it's a little . . . rare for me."

He flicked his tail, making a chuff-chuff sound, before his limbs quivered, shifted, and morphed into a very naked tall, muscular human.

"Elijah?" I stammered.

This couldn't be right. Animals didn't transform into humans, especially not into a man I was crushing on hard in real life.

"Yes, my Hope," he uttered in a dark, masculine voice.

Electricity sparked in my body as my eyes perused his mouthwatering splendor. His short, thick black hair had hints of gold, and his beard was well groomed. But it was his stunning but strange amber eyes with gold flecks that always made my stomach flip-flop, like a fish out of water. His eyes were the windows to his soul. They bored into me with an intensity that made my sex clench.

"Damn. Even in my dream . . . you're fucking splendid," I declared. My eyes trailed down his hard body to his engorged, perfect shaft standing at attention.

He clutched my face between his enormous, calloused hands. "Eyes up here, darling." His face dissolved into an exquisite grin. "Unless you're finally ready to get on all fours for your big kitty?" His hands dropped away and grabbed me around the waist, yanking me against his naked body.

"My, you're such a dirty pussycat, and I love it." I licked his bottom lip.

"So that's a yes." It was a statement, not a question.

"Baby, I'll do whatever you want . . . however you want. But only if you promise to lick all my cream, like a good kitty."

We stared at each other with my legs straddling one of his rock-solid thighs.

"There's nothing good about me, darling, but I can promise to lick you to the very last drop." His voice was thick with emotion. "Just say when, my beautiful mate."

EXCERPT: CLAIMED BY HER TWO ALPHAS

Want to sample a new series? Check out my Shifter Alphas Furever books including this book, <u>Claimed by Her Two Alphas</u>.

In the two weeks since that conversation with Peyton, one snippet of that bizarre conversation kept running through my head. These guys were looking for their perfect *mate*. Not mates, plural. Not one guy wanting one and the other guy wanting... something else. Both guys were looking for the same thing, and according to Alex, that thing was me. But I was only one woman and even if I'd gotten past the weirdness of two guys wanting to share one blind date, I still hadn't wrapped my head around how I could be the perfect mate for both of them.

Yet here I was, trying to figure out how I was going to find not just one, but two blind dates in a crowded bar. I should have backed out.

No. You shouldn't have. It's not going to kill you to do this. If it backfires, you can tell Peyton "I told you so."

At least I should have figured out some way to recognize these guys, like carrying a rose or wearing a bow in my hair. Or maybe a name tag, so instead of standing in the crowd turning in useless circles, I could find these guys. I made another sweep of the room.

You're overthinking...just take a breath and let go.

I closed my eyes, wavering slightly in my heels, did my best imitation of someone poised and collected, and concentrated on my breathing. Then I opened my eyes. The crowd parted and there he was. Or there *some* guy was, some really handsome guy.

He was sitting at the bar, and he was looking right at me. For a split second I thought I'd made him up, or maybe I'd hallucinated him out of desperation. Even sitting down, he was big and broad-shouldered, taking up more physical space than anyone around him. Or maybe he just looked like he was. He should have been imposing, scary, but he radiated an all-American boy kind of feel, the hunky guy-next-door who helped you with your groceries or changed the flat on your car. *A nice, safe guy.*

Until I got to his eyes. Blue. Even in the dim light of the bar, I could tell they were blue. The all-American hunk had just turned the tiniest bit dangerous. There was a fire in those eyes that woke up something deep and primal, something I'd thought didn't exist in me. Or at least I'd never experienced it. I wouldn't go as far as calling it love at first sight; lust at first sight, maybe. Whatever it was, it was pretty amazing.

I really wanted to take a step forward, but I was rooted in place. His eyes held mine, never looking away, and it was like a magnet, drawing me closer. Something held me back though.

But wait...what about my date? Just because this guy likes looking at me...and I like looking at him...

I turned away, the act of breaking away from his gaze doing nothing to lessen the heat that had built up inside me. I was supposed to be here looking for my mystery men, not falling for the first guy who caught my eye.

Turn around...what if it's him?

That thought came out of the blue. And for once, I listened to the voice in my head and did a slow turn. The guy was smiling at me, and something inside me simultaneously clenched and loosened up. It was a physical sensation, a thud deep and low, and I took a step back, shocked by my body's reaction.

When he stood, I saw just how tall he was, well over six feet. He cut easily through the crowd toward me with a grace that belied his size. He stopped just in front of me, and I looked up into those piercing blue eyes.

"Hi, Sadie. I'm Dane. Dane Hastings."

I stared. Just plain unattractively, open-mouthed, deer-in-headlights stared at this amazing specimen, who'd just told me he was one half of my blind date. Saints preserve me, maybe I'd gotten lucky. Then it hit me.

Where the hell was the other guy?